# Murder

# In

# Care

## Nicholas E Watkins

# The Eastbourne Murders Series

## Murder Most Christian

## Murder Lost in Time

## About the Author

Nicholas Watkins lives on the South Coast and is the Author of the Tim Burr series of spy novels. He has four children. He worked as an accountant for many years in the City of London.

Murder in Care

# Chapter 1

"You doing all the right things, Miss Thorndyke. It is not an easy time for anyone especially in the care sector dealing with the elderly," said Dr Passmore. He had finished his rounds at the Hill View Residential Home and was packing his medical bag.

"It is the lack of personal protective equipment that gives me the biggest headache. I spend most of my time now on the phone chasing supplies," she replied. "I swear the last few weeks since the outbreak of this coronavirus have put years on me." She was fishing for a complement. She was a very attractive women in her late thirties or early forties.

"Nonsense, you look remarkable," he rose to the bait and smiled at her.

She began to speak when there was a knock on her office door. It opened and a young woman in a white overall entered without waiting.

"What is it Elvira?" said Tiny Thorndyke somewhat miffed at the untimely interruption.

"I was wondering if Dr Passmore had a few minutes to have a look at Mr Nightingale before he leaves?" Elvira Mercado had come from the Philippines and had worked at the care home for nearly three years. Her accent remained but her language skills were impeccable. She had obviously had a good education but could only find work in the care sector.

"What's the problem?" said Dr Passmore.

"He cut himself and I think it has become infected?"

"I'll be along in a moment," he said.

"He is in the lounge," said Elvira as she left.

The home had eighteen residents in total. Most of whom had gathered in the lounge waiting for lunch to be served when Dr Passmore entered wearing a surgical mask and a plastic apron. He looked around and saw Elvira waiting near the French widows that overlooked the garden. He made his way across the room to her.

John Nightingale was sat on the window seat alongside another resident June Pulford. Elvira stood. "I understand you have a cut?" said Dr Passmore as he approached.

"It's just a scratch," said John.

"Let me have a look then." John raised his hand revealing a gash. It was clearly inflamed and infected. "Well I shall prescribe a course of antibiotics. Make sure you complete the course."

As he spoke June, who had been sitting quietly beside him suddenly got to her feet and marched across the room to greet another elderly woman who had just entered. She began to shout. "How dare you, how dare you?"

The new arrival, Sybil Meadows was taken aback by the verbal onslaught that confronted her. She seemed confused by the anger June was aiming at her. "I don't understand.."

"Don't come the innocent with me," screamed June Pulford. "I know you accused him."

"Who, I don't know what you are on about?"

"For your information John wouldn't take anything, you bitch."

Elvira dashed  across the lounge and put herself between them. "Stop this now," she said. "June go and sit back down. Sybil let's go and sit over here," She led Sybil to the other side of the room as June reluctantly made her way back to Dr Passmore and John Nightingale by the window.

The doctor decided that he did not want to become involved in the altercation. As June approached red faced with anger, he said. "I have left my medical bag in the office. I'll go back, write the prescription and give it to to Miss Thorndyke to get filled." His speedy exit was thwarted however by the appearance of Tiny Thorndyke carrying his bag.

Tina Thorndyke and Dr Thomas Passmore stood in the lobby. "Well that was a bit dramatic, he said.

"There are always squabbles here. It is living in close proximity day in and day out. Tensions are bound to build."

"I shan't be able to visit for a while. It is too risky with the virus spreading."

It was clear that Tina was disappointed and it showed in her face. "But..." she began to speak.

"It is difficult for everyone," he interrupted her and smiled. She nodded and reached out and touched his hand. Elvira watched quietly from the hallway where she had been for some while. "it changes nothing, trust me," he said. He turned and headed for his car parked on the driveway.

She watched him drive off and became aware of a movement in the bushes at the side of the building. She could clearly see a small cloud of smoke rising up. She marched across the drive towards the foliage. "What are you doing?" she shouted.

Tom started and quickly dropped the cigarette. "I, I," he started to speak.

"Don't bother," she said. "Just get back to the kitchen and get on with preparing lunch." Tom acted as a sort of gardener come handyman. He was not ideal but you got what you paid for and Tina did not like to pay a lot.

She turned to go back inside when she heard the sound of a car turning into the drive. Stephenie Foster was at the wheel, Sybil's daughter. At leat she was on her own and not with the pompous arse of a husband, Jeffrey. Tina found him insufferable. He had been some sort of medic in the army and had a habit of criticising everything at the Home. He was a nuisance and a know all.

"My Mum called. She seemed upset," said Stephenie stepping from the car.

"It was nothing," said Tina.

"It didn't sound like nothing to me? She said she had been attacked by June Pulford."

"It was a minor argument. It is over now."

"I want to see her."

"You know that's not possible under the social distancing rules. It is difficult but we need to stick to the Government Guidelines. You can talk over the phone an so on."

She reluctantly accepted the situation but she had to make some form of statement anyway. "I have brought her some vitamins and supplement. My husband Jeffrey says they will strengthen her immune system. We worry about the adequacy of the diet here.

"Of course you do, " said Tina under her breath, then louder, "Just leave them there and I'll see she gets them." Stephenie opened the boot of the car and reluctantly left them. She got back in the car and drove off.

# Chapter 2

"Shouldn't you be at home or something?" said Mandy.

"Why would that be?" asked Sam.

"Well," Mandy paused realising that she had entered the area known as digging a hole and at this point she knew that she should throw away the shovel. However she kept on digging seeing no way of avoiding an answer as Sam gave her his full attention. "Well I was concerned for you welfare." she said lamely.

"Why would that be?" Sam raised his eyebrows quizzically.

"I mean with the coronavirus.."

"Yes I have heard of it."

"Well you could be in the more vulnerable group.."

"Elderly, you mean?"

"No of course not, sort of oldish," Mandy at this point was praying for something to happen, an earthquake, hurricane, the second coming anything that would divert the conversation. Sadly there was no intervention and she saw the hole she was digging reaching cavern proportions.

"I see," said Sam.

"I didn't mean that," said Mandy.

"What do you want me to do? Sit at home? I've been a copper all my life. I don't know anything else. If I go and hide behind closed doors I don't think the criminals will do the same. Do you? I can still do some good even if you think I am past it."

"I don't think your past it. I didn't say that. I was just concerned that's all."

Sam laughed. This Mandy found slightly confusing. Sam's default setting was curmudgeonly and laughter was not one of the options on his remote. "I know," he said. "But we will stick to the distancing rules and hope for the best. I am not that old and not in a high risk group, so do not fear."

Mandy watched as the hole grew smaller. Changing the subject slightly she opened the box on her desk. "We all have a nice packet of personal protection gear. In addition to the usual gloves and bits we now have upgraded face masks to wear."

Sam with drew his mask from his pocket and started to put it on. "That's upside down," she said. Sam muttered something under his breath and finally moulded the mask to his face.

"What we actually need is testing. We can't keep the distance between us in the squad car," he said.

"No chance of that. There are not even enough kits to test the Doctors and nurses in hospitals. So we will be well down the list and sometime before we get tested. We shall just have to make do and hope."

Sam left her office to see what resources she had to hand apart from Detective Sergeant Sam Shaw. She was supposed to have three Detective Constables, Merryweather, Potts and Siskin. She now had Siskin. Keeping her distance she approached. "Merryweather and Potts," she asked?

"Morning boss," he looked up. "They are self isolating."

"Well at least social distancing won't be an issue," she mused.

"It's quiet at the moment anyway," he said.

"i am guessing the number of domestics will rise as we get further into self isolating. Nothing like being stuck indoors to bring out the murderer in the family."

"True but they don't take a lot of solving," smiled Siskin. "The husband or the wife did it."

"There is that I suppose, anything else?" she asked.

"Not a dickey, I am just tidying up old files and neglected paperwork."

Mandy returned to her office and sat looking out the window. She observed Sam, at his desk playing with his face mask. He had decided that paperwork could wait. In fact paperwork could always wait with Sam. Sam's approach to paperwork was to put it off indefinitely and hope he retired before it caught up with him. She saw him pick up the phone and hold a brief conversation before getting up and heading in her direction.

"We have a murder," he said.

"Where and how?" said Mandy.

"Well not so much a murder as an anonymous call concerning a suspicious death."

"Where?" Mandy repeated.

"In a care home."

Mandy's enthusiasm drained from her face. "Right, a care home, elderly residents and coronavirus and one has died?" she said.

"That's about the gist of it."

"Any information the caller that reported the so called suspicious death?"

"Nothing, the call was made from the home itself. The phone is available to all the staff and residents. Could have been any number of people."

"Not a lot of credibility then. I would assume there are a number of residents that have not only health but mental issues. Too many Agatha Christi readers under one roof is my guess."

"Well we still need to investigate," said Sam seizing on the opportunity to avoid paperwork.

It was rare to have spare time but crime had fallen. With empty roads and pavements the average criminal was finding it difficult to ply their trade. Shops were controlling the footfall making life hard for the shoplifters. The lack of people out at night was slowing the muggers and the closed bars reduced the drunks to zero and in consequence assaults and grievous bodily harm cases.

"Okay we will check it out," said Mandy.

There was little to be done on social distancing in the car as they drove along. "Where are we going?"

Sam was driving, "The Hill View Residential Home," he said. "It is a very posh one for the wealthy. Sort of five star luxury for the elderly, lots of facilities."

They headed towards the outskirts of Eastbourne, west towards Brighton. On a hill overlooking the bay Sam drove the car through the gates, passed lawn and flower beds and came to a halt outside a faux

Gothic style mansion built in the Victorian era. "Looks like a boarding school or a nunnery," said Mandy as they stepped from the car.

"Right on both accounts, it has been used as both over the years," said Sam.

They put on their face masks as they approached the door. They waited outside and rang the bell. Normally they would have made their way to reception but times had changed. They had phoned ahead and warned the home of their impending visit.

"DCI Pile," asked the woman who opened the door. "I am Tina Thorndyke, can you tell me what this is about?"

# Chapter 3

"I am DCI Pile and this is DS Shaw," said Mandy to overcome Tina's assumption that the older male was the most senior of them. They stood outside the Hill View Residential Care Home adhering to the social distancing rules.

"I see. So what can I do for you DCI Pile?"

"We have had a report of a death taking place here?"

Tina looked slightly perplexed. "You are aware that this is a home for the elderly? I assume you have been watching the news and have heard of coronavirus? So I think whilst sad, death among the elderly of the virus is not uncommon. It is the new norm. We have done better than most here. I have put considerable effort in obtaining protective equipment and our policy of no one in and no one out has in the main proved successful."

"No one in or out?" Said Sam.

"The staff live on site and are in lock down with the residents and no one is allowed onto the premises. Supplies are delivered and left outside. We have in effect managed to self isolate the home from the outside world."

"No one at all comes in?"

"Dr Passmore has been our only visitor for the past weeks."

"Surely he must pose a high risk to the elderly residents?" said Mandy.

"We observe the same practice as they do in hospitals. Before entering Dr Passmore, disinfects, and dons full PPE. The risk of transmission, he assures me is minimal. In any event the residents still need attention for their various medical conditions, some of which need regular monitoring and treatment. There is little point in preventing the spread of the virus if they die of their existing conditions through lack of treatment,is there?"

Sam somewhat taken aback by Tina's comprehensive reply said, "Er no suppose not."

Mandy spoke, "and yet you have a death?"

"We do. I cannot see why that would raise suspicion in anyone. The deceased was eighty nine."

"The deceased?"

"Sybil Meadows," said Tina.

"What was the cause of death?"

"Coronavirus.."

"And yet you operate this no one in and no one out policy," said Sam.

"She must have made contact somehow. Dr Passmore is looking at everything to try and find out how she became infected," said Tina.

"Are the other residents showing symptoms?"

"Not that we can tell. We do, as I said practice total social distancing and so hope to minimise minimise the risk of transmission between the residents. Crossed fingers we seem to have been successful, this far. What we need is testing of course. At the moment we have no way of knowing who as it or who has recovered from it. The Government keep promising but nothing happens."

"So as I see it," Sam looked at his notes. "This Sybil Meadows is the only death and your only coronavirus case?"

"Yes, we have been fortunately. When I say fortunately I take some small credit for the rapid introduction of the measures to protect the staff and residents alike."

"Who certified the death?" said Mandy.

"Dr Passmore, he was in attendance when she died."

"She didn't go to hospital?" said Sam.

Tina gave him that look that indicated that she found his question naïve. "There are pressures on the National health Service. She would occupy an intensive care bed with no chance of survival. There is no official policy but we in the Care sector are fully aware that elderly coronavirus patients and being shipped back into the care homes to die and free up ICU beds. It just spreads the virus."

As they spoke the sound of car could be heard in the distance. Tina

Thorndyke looked at her watch. "Ah, that will be Dr Passmore. It is his visiting day. So you can ask him yourself."

They watched as a middle aged man with greying hair stepped from the Mercedes he had parked on the drive. He looked every inch the part of your local family doctor. Observing the the social distancing rules Tina introduced him to the police.

Standing two metres apart the conversation continued. "I understand you attended Mrs Meadows, Doctor," said Mandy.

"That is correct. Why is there a problem?"

"Someone contacted the station and said that she died in suspicious circumstances," added Sam.

"We are duty bound to follow up," said Mandy.

"I see," said Dr Passmore. "Well I can assure you that her death was of natural causes, or at least what passes for natural causes in these difficult times."

"And you issued the death certificate, May I ask the cause of death?"

"Heart failure, following respiratory infection."

"Pneumonia?" said Sam.

"Pneumonia," confirmed Dr Passmore.

"Is there anything else?" asked Tina.

"No, I can't say there is," said Mandy.

Sitting in the car, driving along the seafront Sam spoke, "Well that was a waste of time. Seems like some old biddy at the care home, with an over active imagination made the anonymous call reporting the murder."

"it would appear so, There is little to investigate especially with her doctor attending and certifying the death."

They made their way back to the incident room. "Anything?" she called to Siskin.

"Not a bean, quiet as the grave."

She made her way to the office and started on the pile of paperwork which seemed to increase exponentially in inverse proportion to the decrease in actual police work. The murder rate was on the up but detective work was on the down. In lock down domestic tensions had naturally risen, some turned violent and some resulted in one spouse murdering the other. However uniform, in the main just needed to pick up the guilty party and there was little to investigate.

She noted that a letter had been delivered. They envelope had been typed and opened. Its contents had been checked for safety before it had been passed to her. It was simply addressed 'Murder in Care.'

Intrigued, Mandy opened the letter and removed the contents. It was a print off a photograph taken on a mobile phone. She began to read. She called out "Sam come here."

Sam wondered into her office and sat opposite. She pushed the printed sheets across the desk. She waited as he read,

"Bugger me," he said.

"Exactly," she said.

The photos were of a Will, Sybil Meadows' will. It was dated the day before her death. It left all her possessions to Dr Passmore.

# Chapter 4

"The pictures of Sybil Meadows' Will were taken on someone's mobile phone and printed off," said Sam. "Is there anyway of telling who took them?"

He and Mandy were studying the five prints left for them. "No there is no indication. If whoever had taken them had emailed them sent via text we could have gathered that data but not from a print out."

"Whoever it is wanted to remain anonymous and knew we would be able to trace back from any electronic communication. I suppose that is the first question that needs an answer. Why, if you suspected a murder, would you want to remain anonymous? Why not just call the police?" said Sam.

"It is odd," admitted Mandy. "Anyway it gives a motive for Dr Passmore to want Sybil dead and a bit more credence to her possible murder."

"We could have a Harold Shipmen, the doctor who murdered twenty odd elderly women and changed their Wills." said Sam. "It could be you first serial killer case. You will be famous like the detective who went after Jack the Ripper, what's his name?"

"That famous, I could be what's her name," laughed Mandy.

"To be honest the Will looks less than convincing, very amateurish," said Sam.

"My thoughts as well. It could just be someone with a grudge against Dr Passmore and wants to stir up a bit of trouble for him. Any of the residents at the Hill View Residential Care Home could have mocked up a Will. Lets face it, they have a lot of time on their hands and tensions are bound to build up between them. Perhaps one of them felt that they weren't getting their fair share of attention from the good doctor and wanted to cause a bit of bother for him. Who knows?"

"There is the name from a firm of local solicitors on the Will though, Trent, Styles and Pilcher."

"They are just up the road from here. We called take a social distance walk and have a chat. Give them a bell and see if there is anyone in?"

Mr Harwood sat at the other end of the conference table and Mandy and Sam at the other. "There are just the two of us in. We are taking it in turns to man the office. Most of the partners and staff are working from home. We are sort of acting as gofers for the rest. We dig out files, correspondence and the like. Scan anything they need and send it to them."

"So are there a Trent, Styles or Pilcher about?" asked Sam.

"No they have been dead donkey's years. I am the senior partner now," said Harwood. "What can I do for you?"

Mandy pushed the photographs of the Will down the desk. Harwood retrieved them wearing surgical gloves. "The new normal, go to work wearing marigolds," he smiled. He glanced at them. "I'll get the file," he said and left the room.

Mandy and Sam sat patiently waiting for his return. He eventually returned after a interval of some fifteen minutes. "I am sorry it took so long. The file was out. I didn't realise that Mrs Meadows was recently deceased. The file was in the process of being dealt with by one of my colleagues from home. I have spoken to him on the phone and I am up to speed on it. What do you want to know?"

"Firstly are those pictures of the Will genuine? That is has her Will been changed in favour of this Dr Passmore?" said Mandy.

"To be honest the change is irrelevant. It does not look genuine and my colleague confirms that Mrs Meadows had not changed her will in favour of Dr Passmore."

"Sorry what do you mean by irrelevant?" said Sam.

"Well Mrs Meadows in a sense had virtually no assets to leave."

"I don't understand the cost of staying at Hill View must be quite an expense. You would need to be fairly wealthy to afford their fees I imagine?" said Mandy.

"Yes substantial indeed around sixty thousand a year from the accounts information I have."

"So?" said Sam.

"Oh I see. Mrs Meadows whist having no income or assets of her own, did have an lifetime interest in her late husbands estate. Which is substantial, somewhere in the region of five or six million pound based on the last valuation."

"I am still unclear. Her husband left her five or six million and yet her estate is worth nothing?"

"It is a trust in essence she can use the money and assets while she still lives, for her maintenance and expenses but she does not own the estate. She was holding it in trust until she died."

"So when she dies what happens?" said Mandy.

"The residue passes to the beneficiaries?"

"Who are?" prompted Sam.

"Oh, hold on." He shuffled the papers in front of him. "Ah, here it is, Matthew Meadows and Stephenie Meadows." He sat back. "So Dr Passmore won't have anything coming his way and in any event this purported will is a crude forgery at best. I have Mrs Meadows will here."

"Who are Matthew and Stephenie?" said Mandy.

Harwood again shuffled through the papers. "You have to understand I do not normally deal with Wills, Probate etcetera. My area is more in the realm of conveyancing. Have it, Matthew is Mr Meadows son from his previous marriage and Stephanie is the issue of his union with Sybil Meadows."

"Is his his first wife still alive?" asked Mandy.

Harwood undertook the now familiar paper shuffling before answering. "No," he said finally.

"And?" said Sam.

"Oh, she died many years ago. Mr Meadows was a widower when he married Sybil."

"And Matthew and Stephenie Meadows do you have their whereabouts?"

"We have no idea where Mr Matthew Meadows is, he apparently disappeared many years ago losing contact with his step mother. Her daughter lives her in Eastbourne." He gave Sam her address which he noted in his note book.

"And they are the only people that would realistically benefit from

Sybil Meadows death?"

"Now she is dead they receive the balance of the life time trust set up by their father," more paper shuffling. "This might be of interest to you though. Over the last few months Mrs Meadows has transferred a considerable amount of money from the trust," he paused and noted down and totalled some figures on a piece of paper. "Um that is quite a bit and way outside her normal pattern of spending."

"How much are we talking about?" said Sam.

"From my figures just short of four hundred and fifty thousand."

Sam whistled, "as you say, that is quite a bit in anybodies book."

"And that this is trust money, what about here own will?" said Mandy.

"Just odds and sods, bits and pieces of jewellery left as mementoes to old friends nothing worth killing for," said Harwood. He paused, "Hold on, she left twenty thousand to a  Elvira Mercado. I think she must be a nurse at High View."

"So where where did the four hundred and fifty grand go?" asked Sam.

# Chapter 5

Superintendent Taylor's less than cheerful face appeared on Mandy's laptop screen as she sat in her office at the police station. Sam stood just out of camera shot concealed from his gaze. "What is this about?" he asked.

Mandy was unclear in her own mind as to how she would sell this one to her boss. It was clear that Taylor was not in a happy place. He had been in self imposed isolation for over a week and being trapped at home was clearly not agreeing with him. Mandy knew to a great extent that she was not one of the Superintendent's most favourite people. He had social and career aspirations. Like most aspects of British society class came into play The classic maxim of who you knew and not what you knew was just as true in the Police as in other institutions. He was well aware that Mandy and been to a top public school, university and that her parents were well connected. Despite the fact that Mandy had never traded on this, Taylor was still uncomfortable with her upper class roots and was inherently suspicious. He knew Mandy was a good copper but he could not totally overcome his inherent prejudice.

DS Sam Shaw on the other hand just saw her as posh. Coming to the end of his time on the force and heading for retirement, he just accepted it for what it was. It gave him something to moan about. She had the brains and he had the street smarts. She had the flair and he had the experience.

"I think there may have been a murder?" she began.

Taylor's expression was one of, 'here we go again.' He did not react initially and his face just looked back sternly from her laptop screen. He finally spoke. "Is this to do with the death at High View?"

"It is .." she failed to finish her sentence before he interrupted.

"I have read the notes," he emphasised the word read and to label the point continued. "I have read the notes thoroughly. Correct me if I am wrong but the attending doctor completed the death certificate certifying natural causes, did he not?"

"Yes ..,"

"And again, correct me if I am wrong none of us are qualified as medical practitioners, as far as I am aware, are we?"

"No..,"

"Then given that the deceased was old, had medical problems and died of natural causes as far as her doctor was concerned, who I might add is qualified, why are you still spending time on this?"

Mandy realised that she was not making the best case for resources to be allocated to the case. She took a deep breath and tried again. "Money seems to have gone missing, around four hundred odd thousand and there seems to have been an attempt to forge a will."

"That may or may not be the case but it does not make it murder. If there has been fraud or attempted fraud we must assume that it will be reported in due course by her relatives. You are making assumptions. If and when the matter is reported to the police the fraud team, I am sure are quite up to dealing with the matter. You have to accept that she died of natural causes."

Mandy realised that Taylor was correct. All she had to back up her suspicion was an anonymous phone call, a photograph of a poor attempt to fake Sybil Meadow's Will and a conversation with her solicitors, who had flagged an unusual spending pattern prior to her death.

Weighing against this was the fact that she was old and infirm and was receiving regular treatment from Dr Passmore, who had signed her death certificate. More telling was the fact the care home was in lock down. The people who benefited most from her death, those who inherited under the Will, had no access to the deceased.

She had no real response. Sam had remained silent to this point, off camera. "Hello Governor," he moved into camera range.

"Sam how are you? Should you not be isolating?" said Taylor.

"I am not that bleeding old. I have a few years left in me yet, so quit with the ageism," he laughed which was a rare sight for Sam.

Taylor smiled back. "So what do you make of all this?"

"I am with you Sir. Load of all toffee as far as I can see but I have a lot of respect for DC Pile. She has been pretty on the money in the past so I am not in any rush to dismiss the matter."

A slight look of concern spread across Taylor's face. He knew Sam had been around the block a few times. You did not spend as long as he in the job without having a nose for things. "So what's your take?"

"Well as I said I am in total agreement with you assessment but.." he let the sentence hang and watch the doubt build in the superintendent's demeanour before continuing. "We don't want a Harold Shipmen on our hands do we. It has now come to light that he was the biggest serial killer this Country has ever had. If you recall the Police Force involved had numerous opportunities to investigate him, suspicions where raised many times. Each time the reports were ignored. If I remember correctly, he murdered his elderly patients and certified there deaths as natural."

"Of course I am aware of the case, the whole Country is. What's your point, Sam?"

"As I recall the enquiry that followed highlighted the failings of the police in the matter. I have never heard much subsequently about the officers that were in charge at the time. I doubt that it did a great deal for their career prospects though. I don' t suppose you know what happened to them?"

Mandy watched as Taylor mulled it over. He knew exactly what happens to Officers that balls up. They are sidelined and put where they can do no further harm. He certainly did not want his career to tread that path. "So what's your take on it?"

Sam said, "you are probably right and we there is no point in pursuing it further. I shall make a note on the file that you were consulted and kicked it into the long grass. We can then get on with some proper police work."

"Let's not be too hasty. Pile has a good record in these matters and as her DS you should realistically support her when she gets these instincts in a case." He paused.

Speaking to Mandy, " I am less than convinced but as Shaw says we don't want this force becoming the subject of an enquiry down the road. So what is you want?"

Sam winked at Mandy and she almost laughed. She had to admire her DS. While siding against her with Taylor, he had managed to convince the Superintendent that he should support her by sowing the seed that if things went wrong, it would be his career prospects that were on the line.

"I think we should request an autopsy and just check the cause of Sybil Meadow's death. If you think that would be the wise thing to do?"

"That's what I want. As DS Shaw said. We don't want another Shipmen do we?"

"Certainly not Sir, not worth throwing careers away."

"Quite so," said Taylor and logged off.

"You are a very sneaky man, DS Sam Shaw," laughed Mandy.

"A posh education doesn't teach you everything," he muttered as he wandered out of her office.

# Chapter 6

"Siskin," called Mandy adhering to social distancing and saving herself a walk from her office to his desk in the process. "I need you to do some digging."

"Shovel ready, boss," he replied.

"Right, first I want you to find out as much as you can about the doctor at the care home, Passmore. He practices privately and specialises in the care of the elderly. You will need to get his disciplinary record with the British Medical Association or whoever is his regulator. Then see if there have been any unusual events in his career."

"Like what?" said Siskin.

"Like him bumping off elderly patients and inheriting under their Wills."

"Right, how am I supposed to do that?"

"I am sure you will find a way. In any event get his financial records, personal and his medical practice and go through them."

"Anything else?" -

"Tina Thorndyke, the owner of High View find out all you can. Get her history. Find out what money she has or doesn't have. "

"You do know that I am the only one here," said Siskin.

"Yep I had noticed. Get Merryweather and Potts linked into the Police Computer system at home and get them working on it too. They only have mild symptoms the last I heard."

"We are working on it," he replied.

"And.."

"And..," said Siskin.

"And I need everything you can dig up on Sybil's daughter Stephenie, her husband and her stepson from her husbands' first marriage, Matthew Meadows."

Siskin was looking less than enamoured at the mounting list of tasks Mandy had given him. "Anything else, while I am at it?"

"No that you remind me, yes. I want a list of all employees at the High View and a criminal record check run on them."

Siskin set to his tasks. Sam entered her office. "You do know we don't even know there has been a crime committed, don't you."

"Do you think her death was natural?" she asked Sam. "What does your gut tell you?"

"Sam hesitated before replying. "Alright I agree, something is not right but I can't say it is murder though."

"We will get the autopsy report in a day or two and that will answer the question. In the meantime let's do a bit of digging."

"Well let's start with Dr Passmore, shall we?"

Ten minutes later she and Sam settled down in front of the computer screen. "This is all a bit different. It is like going to the pictures," he said.

Mandy pressed the button and waited for Dr Passmore to answer the Skype call. "Pictures?" she said. "I do wonder what era you are living in, sometimes."

"Pictures, flicks, cinema, all the same."

"It gets worse, flicks?"

"They film flickers doesn't?"

Dr Passmore's face filled the screen. "Good afternoon," said Mandy. "Thank you for responding to my request so rapidly for an interview."

"Only to glad to help," he replied.

"Since we met at High View there been a number of developments. I should like to get you comments on them if that is okay?

"As I said I am only too happy to help."

"I have sent a copy of a document that has come into our possession. Do you have it?"

"The Will of Sybil Meadows. I do. It is clearly a forgery. I have never seen before."

"You have no idea of its origin?" said Mandy.

"None, it is certainly nothing to do with me, if that is what you are asking?"

"Can you think of any reason why anyone would forge such a document?"

"It is beyond my comprehension. It is a blatant attempt to set me up."

"That leads me to my next question, why? Can you think of someone who wants to get even, as a grudge or dislikes you for some reason?"

"There are always tensions. A lot of the residents in High View are ageing and not all have full control over their mental capacity. There are endless squabbles and falling outs among the residents and each other, the staff and I may well have somehow become involved without even being aware of it."

"I see. Can you give me a for instance possibly involving Sybil Meadows?"

"Well I am obviously not the best person to ask. Tina Thorndyke would know more of the ins and outs but I am aware there was a sort of feud going on with two other residents."

"Go on , who specially?"

"Sybil accused another resident of going through her things and stealing, as far as I can recall."

"Do you have a name?"

"John Nightingale, it seemed to escalate and also involved June Pulford. She is, using the term loosely Mr Nightingale's love interest. Apparently there was an almighty flare up between them that has festered over the past month or so. I am sure Ms Thorndyke will be able to fill in more details."

I will ask her. Were there any other tensions that you are aware of?"

"I think she had a falling out with her daughter. I am not clear what it was about. I got the impression it was over money and her daughter's husband. I was there one day and when I left, Sybil and her daughter, Stephenie were shouting at each other in the garden"

"Not all love and harmony at High View then?" she said.

"Far from it I am afraid, " replied Dr Passmore.

"Oh just one other thing. You should know that I have ordered an autopsy into Sybil's death."

She watched his reaction. He looked distinctly uncomfortable. Finally he spoke," I see. Is that all?"

"For now, thank you for your cooperation." The screen went blank.

"Certainly didn't like that," said Sam.

"I am pretty  certain that when we get the report it won't be reading natural causes," said Mandy.

# Chapter 7

Siskin had been busy. He loved a bit of tech and relished digging into the Police and other databases. Having got the go ahead, Sybil Meadows body had been retrieved from the undertakers and moved to the autopsy laboratory. Mandy and Sam had the rest of the team, DCs Potts and Merryweather working from home while Siskin coordinated their efforts Their enquiries were procedure based on the assumption that her death would prove to be unnatural.

Keeping as much distance as was practically possible in the incident room, Mandy approached Siskin's desk. "Anything for me yet," she asked.

"I have just been speaking to the pathologist. I didn't realise how bad this coronavirus is getting. They had trouble retrieving the deceased. Did you know that they have a backlog of burials? The cemeteries and crematoriums just cannot deal with the numbers. It is a nightmare they are running out of chilled storage facilities at mortuaries and funeral parlours. They are using refrigerated trailers usually used for frozen food transport to store the deceased."

"It is a sobering thought," Mandy was truly shocked. "A good time for a murder though with so much death and confusion. The medical profession inundated and resources stretched to the limit. It is the time for evil to flourish."

"Very philosophical," commented Sam as he walked into earshot.

"it is true though. If you are intent on murder you are by definition not the sort of human being that has a great deal of regard or empathy for humanity. They put themselves at the centre and justify murder as their right, their due for a wrong committed or something they feel they have been deprived of. I am not talking about the random act of violence like a punch thrown but of the motivation for calculated murder. They all feel they have had or having something taken from them that gives them the right to kill."

"Domestics?" said Siskin.

Sam replied. "Mostly men, mostly insecure and controlling and can't either accept rejection or the loss of control. The partner is theirs and if they can't have her no one else will."

"When it comes down to it there a very few motives for murder. To escape detection for another crime or murder for example a robbery gone bad. Then there is financial gain say for the life assurance or again robbery. And as you say the controlling spouse."

"You do get the abused partner who snaps after years of abuse," said Siskin.

"It's not really murder is it? It is really self defence except the attack as been spread over years rather than minutes," said Sam.

"So what do you think this is? If there has been a murder?" said Siskin.

"Oh I am sure there has been a murder and it will be for financial gain," said Mandy.

"Well I might be able to help with a motive," said Siskin. "High View is in deep trouble financially. As you may have gleaned it is not a care home as such. It is described as a ' a retreat for the senior members of the community' a 'safe and luxurious retirement environment' a ..."

Sam interrupted, "Okay I get it it a posh retirement gaff."

"In a nutshell. It has a spa, on site cinema and entertainment, a la carte dining and luxury apartments for the residents and so on."

"That doesn't sound cheap. It sounds more like a five star hotel than an old people's home," said Mandy.

"It is extortionate but that does not mean it is profitable. They issue seems to be funding. The resident essentially buys a room and then pay what would be a monthly charge that is set annually."

"A bit like those hotels of that Donald Trump was touting before he got the job of US president. You buy a room in the hotel, with his name on it and then they give you a share of the letting income," said Sam.

"Sort of, except you use the room yourself for a set number of years."

"So the owners of High View get a bundle of cash up front and income from the residents for services provided. Sounds like a money spinner to me," said Sam.

"It should be but of course it relies on the capital being invested and making the projected rate of return and .."

"And that relies on reasonable interest rates and a climbing stock market. Now interest rates are around zero and the market has tanked," said Mandy.

"It was hanging on by a thread until a few months ago. I have had a look at the bank account and guess what?"

"I think I know the answer," joked Sam. "Let me guess around half a million quid has appeared as if by magic?"

"Got it in one," said Siskin.

"Well we know someone who has been spending that sort of money recently, our deceased Sybil Meadows."

"Can you prove the money came from her in High View's bank accounts."

"Not as yet but I am sure I will be able to trace the source of the funds. I am just waiting for the bank to get back."

"We have the first motive for a murder then, financial gain," said Sam.

"Who are the owners of High View?"

"Just Tina Thorndyke," said Siskin.

"Keep digging and get back to me," she said as she and Sam made their way back to her office.

"It is all a bit too easy isn't it," she said as they sat. "You would have to be pretty stupid to steal Sybil's money and then bump her off to cover it up. Wouldn't you?"

"Most murderers aren't that smart, just greedy and most think they are cleverer than anyone else. They do in the main over estimate their own intellect," said Sam.

"I suppose that she could have intended to just borrow the money initially. After all the stock market was climbing until the virus hit and the market crashed after lock down. She probably thought she could pay it back then it just spiralled out of control."

"The pandemic gave her the perfect cover to kill her. Who would think twice about another death in a old people's home?"

"You forget the doctor, he would need to be very incompetent complacent to not notice a murder."

"Well he isn't stupid," said Sam.

"So if she was murdered then his must have been party to it. That rather begs the question as to his motive."

"Well there was the forged Will he was the beneficiary."

"It was a very amateurish attempt though. Dr Passmore is an educated man. I do not think for one minute he would have attempted anything so crude."

"Its not making much sense however you look at it. Even if she wasn't murdered what could be the motive for the production of such a rubbish fake Will?"

"Well the only clear motive we have at he moment is that Thorndyke seems to have had her hand in the decease's pocket. If she murdered Sybil then perhaps the Will is her attempt to cast suspicion on Dr Passmore. Except that would be stupid by necessity he needed to be party to it, as he certified her death as natural causes."

"We need to talk to Tina Thorndyke and Dr Passmore again," said Sam.

"We need the autopsy report. That is what we need," said Mandy.

# Chapter 8

"A new dawn, a new day and a sea of happy faces," said Mandy as she walked into the incident room.

"Morning boss," said Merryweather, then Potts and finally Siskin. Sam grunted and carried on drinking his coffee and eating a bacon roll.

"All fit and well?"

Potts replied first. "Not very fit after fourteen days sat on my backside indoors but clear of the virus."

"Same here," said Merryweather. "Getting back to work probably saved you lot having to investigate a murder. My partner and I felt we were pretty close a number of times. We just couldn't decide who should murder whom."

"Well it's good to have a full squad but we don't have a murder at the moment," said Mandy.

"Go and have a look on your desk. The lab report is back." Said Sam. Having spoken, he went back to eating and reading a newspaper.

Mandy went to her office and re-emerged less than a minute later. "Gather round.."

"Don't bloody gather round me. Stay six foot away. I don't want your germs. And while you are at it, stay six foot from the boss. I have to sit in a car with her."

"Six foot?" said Siskin.

"Old school, two metres and he still reads things printed on paper," replied Merryweather.

"Attention please, we are investigating the murder of Sybil Meadows in High View Residential Home for the elderly. For those you weren't here. We received an anonymous phone call saying that she had been murdered. This was followed by a Will posted here, again anonymously that seem to implicate the doctor who treated her and certified her death. The Will was a poor forgery but the murder was not," said Mandy.

"I am assuming that she was poisoned?" said Sam.

Mandy refereed to the autopsy report. "Arsenic poisoning administered as one fatal dose. No evidence of prolonged ingestion, no other injuries to the deceased."

"This is not going to be easy," said Potts. "I assume that given she is in a Home then more or less anyone could have slipped her the poison, that is anyone who had access to the care home?"

"The first thing we need to do, is to try and find out how it was administered. She died in the morning so we can at assume that she took it within a short period of her death," said Mandy.

Sam grunted, "that is easier said than done. She may have taken it shortly before she died but that doesn't mean it was given to her by the killer at that point. The arsenic could have been in anything she consumed on the morning of her death, her breakfast, her morning coffee, the medication she was on or just some sweets. Anyone at any time could have put the poison in anything she would consume at some point."

"Poisoning has always been tricky," said Siskin. "You don't know when so you can't put anyone in the frame at the time of death."

"We have two things going for us," said Mandy. "I did not think I would be saying this but the coronavirus is actually our friend on this occasion. High View was in lock down. So we have a finite list of suspects."

"And two?" asked Potts.

"Well an assumption really, in that our murderer had a motive. Logically and statically it would be almost beyond probability that High View is home to a geriatric serial killer. So we need to dig and find that motive. We know the how, poisoning and the motive will give us the who. Then we just need to prove it." said Mandy.

She looked at her team and saw scepticism staring back at her. "Oh come on," said Sam. "It is two yards not a couple of metres..."

"What are you on about, Sarge?" said Siskin.

"Old school, feet and inches, no DNA, no forensics, no CCTV, no

AMPR just proper police work," he smiled. " you will need to get up from you digitally enhanced video world that surrounds your desks and ask questions, piece it together and deduce. The clue is in our job descriptions, detectives."

"Sam is right, any comments?" said Mandy.

"What's a yard? I thought it was American for your garden" said Merryweather.

"Thirty six inches," said Sam. "A cricket pitch is twenty two yards or sixty six feet and that is called a chain, the old drop out area on a rugby pitch was a chain as well. There are one hundred links to a chain or four rods. So obviously there are ten chains to a furlong which is an eighth of a mile. So there are eighty chains to a mile and obviously that makes one thousand, seven hundred and sixty yards."

"What are you talking about?" said Siskin. "What happened to kilometres and kilogrammes."

Mandy said, " Sam's point is that like decimal numbers, which are simple to multiply but far too difficult to divide by anything that doesn't end in five or nought, because they leave a remainder, a loose end. We need to tie up those loose ends. Old school, interview, use our brains, check every detail and bear down on the who and why. We have the technology to help but this is good old fashioned detective work and deduction."

"Siskin dig into everything you can on Dr Passmore and Ms Thorndyke. Potts you are on our victim. Sybil Meadows find out everything, she had done, who she knows, whee she has been. She was murdered for a reason and that reason will be part of her life. Merryweather you are on the people who benefit by her death, Stephenie her daughter and husband  Jeffrey Foster, Matthew Meadows her stepson and this care worker whom, she left some money to, Elvira Mercado."

"Sam and I are going back to High View. Now we know we have a murder we need to speak to everyone that had contact with our victim."

"And remember stay at least eighteen hands apart," said Sam.

# Chapter 9

Mandy and Sam sat in the library in the High View. They had  full protective equipment on and satanised everything before setting up. One thing had to be said for Tina Thorndyke she had taken every precaution to protect the elderly residents from the coronavirus that had killed so many in other retirement homes.  Before coming they had consulted with the police surgeon in order to establish exactly the precautions needed to minimise the risk of transmission. The murder of Sybil Meadows had to be investigated but not at the expense of the lives of the other residents.

They decided that the starting point for the investigation was to be the owner of the care home, Tina Thorndyke. Sam opened the questioning. "Since last speaking to you a number of facts have come to light, not least of which is that Mrs Meadows was murdered by poisoning."

"What are you saying? Sybil was murdered?" Tina seemed shocked and raised her voice.

"The first thing we need to ensure is that there are no more poisonings, so we expect your full cooperation," said Mandy.

"Tell me who would want her dead?" said Sam.

Tina paused before replying. "I honestly can't think of anyone."

"It is a confined community under lock down. People are trapped with each other. Don't tell me that tensions have not built up between the residents, the staff, residents and staff. That doesn't ring true," said Mandy.

Sam continued. "Did Mrs Meadows have any enemies, falling outs, family arguments. Things of that nature?"

"Well there was the argument with her daughter Stephenie. Not that I was listening.."

"Of course not but you could not help but overhear," said Sam.

"Precisely, in any event it was about two weeks ago. Stephenie's husband.."

"Can you give us their names?"

"Stephanie and Jeffrey Foster," she replied. "Obviously they had to remain socially distanced so the conversation took place at the rear french windows, Stephanie in the garden and Sybil indoors. From what I heard, in passing of course, was that Jeffrey's business had run into problems and Stephanie was attempting to persuade her mother to lend them some money."

"What precisely was said?"

"Well, Sybil was really angry and quite unkind. She was telling her daughter that her so called husband's business was a joke. Words to the effect that he was just a gambler who had already lost over two hundred thousand pounds of her money. Her exact words were ' not a penny more, not over my dead body'. Stephanie was crying. It was clear that she was desperate. "

"How so, did she say anything?"

"She had lots to say alright. She said that the money was rightly hers, that her father had left it in trust and that she had no right to keep controlling her with the purse strings. Sybil replied that Jeffrey was a layabout that was no better than a pimp living off her."

"Were any threats made?"

"Sybil said that Stephanie would have to wait until she was dead before she had any more money."

"What did her daughter say to that?"

"She stormed off and shouted something to the effect that it might be sooner than she thought."

"What did you make of that?"

"I took it to mean, given her age that she may become a victim of the pandemic."

"Nothing more, you didn't take it as a threat?" said Mandy.

"No of course not, it was just an argument and things get said."

"Did Stephanie have any subsequent meetings with her mother?"

"No she had no close contact if that is what you are suggesting and certainly no way of administering arsenic." she paused and reconsidered, "oh I suppose there are the vitamins."

"The vitamins?" said Sam.

"Stephenie drops around once a month and leaves these health supplements for her mother. She is into all this healthy eating, natural remedies and all that sort of thing."

"Do you give them to her mother and does she take them?"

"I do if I remember. I am not sure if she bothers to take them though?"

"Were there any other tensions in High View?"

"There was an incident with one of the other residents," said Tina. "Sybil accused him of taking stuff from her room."

"And had he?"

"Well nothing was missing, so I suppose not. It did cause a massive argument between them however."

"Name?" said Sam.

"John Nightingale, he hasn't been with us long, so I haven't really got to know him. He does seem very friendly with June Pulford, another resident. She took John's part and almost came to blows with Sybil over it all."

There was an induced silence instigated by Mandy and Sam. When the atmosphere was judged to be sufficiently tense Mandy eventually spoke. "We have been to see Mr Harwood at Trent Styles and Pilcher. Are you familiar with him?"

"I don't think so."

"He is Mrs Meadows' solicitor and will obviously be dealing with her estate. He told us something quite interesting about her recent spending. Do you have any knowledge on this matter?"

There was a long pause before Tina answered. "High View has been experiencing a few cash flow problems. It is asset rich but working capital is an issue."

"That's another way of saying you have run out of money," said Sam bluntly.

"If you prefer, " she was clearly angry. "Anyway as I was saying, I was looking for investment. I discussed the matter with Sybil and she said she would help. She loved the place and was happy to invest. She advanced a sum of money and the paper work was to follow. Things got delayed with the lock down."

"But the money didn't?" She avoided eye contact. "Are you sure that was the situation. On the face of it, it looks like you were just helping yourself to her money?" said Sam.

"I assure you," she was indignant in her response. "I assure it was purely a business arrangement, on commercial terms. It was totally above board."

"And of course now that Mrs Meadows is dead there is no one to contradict you. Is there?" said Mandy.

# Chapter 10

John Nightingale sat opposite Mandy and Sam. He began to speak without being prompted. "Look this is all a load of nonsense. The woman was over reacting."

"What woman are you talking about," soothed Mandy.

"Sybil, Sybil Meadows, of course this is about that nonsense that I was stealing from her, isn't it? I know she is dead and you shouldn't speak ill and so on but, that woman.."

"Go on, what woman what?" said Mandy.

"She had it in for me. She was just waiting to start a row."

"Why would she want to do that?" said Sam.

"Because she was jealous. She was just being vindictive brandishing accusations around."

"I think you need to start from the beginning this is making little sense."

"it all started when I moved into High View.."

"When was that?" asked Mandy.

"What, oh just over two months ago. Anyway it started almost immediately. You see she was really close friends with June."

"That would be Mrs June Pulford?" said Sam checking his list of residents.

"Yes, when I arrived June and I became friends and Sybil felt excluded. It started in a small way. Just comments and little digs but when June didn't take the bait she became more and more petty and nasty."

"Are you telling us that there was some sort of love tryst going on involving the three of you?" said Sam somewhat sceptically.

"No of course not it was just friendship. Old people need company you know. It is not the just the preserve of the young and in your case."

he looked at Sam, "the not so young."

Mandy intervened, "DS Shaw was merely trying to clarify matters and in now way was he passing judgement. What made you pick High View anyway?"

He seemed slightly placated and continued. "I met June on the pier, in Eastbourne in, let me see. It must have been August, no September last year. I think. Anyway we were queuing up at the ice cream parlour at the beginning of the pier and she bought her ice cream, turned, bumped into me and spilt it down me. The rest is history as they say."

"That doesn't explain how you came to be resident here?"

"She told me about the place and I met her a few times. I even came here once or twice. One thing led to another."

"Where were you living before?"

"A flat in by the station."

"You sold it then?"

"It is in the process. The current situation has slowed matters," he said.

"But it is not cheap as I understand the financing here," said Sam.

"Okay I am not a wealthy man and June is helping fund it."

"I see," said Sam.

"You don't see. Life is not all about money." It was clear that a personality clash was an understatement of the dynamic between John and Sam.

Mandy intervened. "What did you do before retiring?"

"I was in the military for a long while, then private security in various Countries Iraq and Africa mostly. Then I moved on to import export, mostly Africa to the Europe."

"What did you import and export?"

"Anything and everything what ever there was a profit in. Age catches up and in the end I came here."

"And you met June and she financed your move to High View?"

"Well it wasn't quite like that but in essence yes."

"Then Sibyl accuses you of stealing because she is put out by your relationship with June?"

"So the relationship was pretty strained between June and Sybil?"

" I should say so. When Dr Passmore was here, thinking about it that was the day before she passed, they almost came to blows in the lounge. It was stupid and childish really."

"I do have one more question. What were you doing in Sybil's room if you were not stealing?"

"I had asked  Elvira to let me in. I had it in my mind to ease the tension between her and June. I had bought her some of her favourite perfume. She had run out and with lock down could get out to buy any. I ordered some on line. I thought it would be a nice surprise. Of course it didn't work out quite like that.  Elvira got bleeped to attend to another resident and Sybil came back. She saw me in her room, holding what she assumed was her expensive perfume and accused me a trying to steal it for June and it escalated from there."

"I assume that," Sam checked his list again. "i assume that this  Elvira Mercado will back up your story?"

"I am sure she will. So there was absolutely no need to call the police. I do think Tina has really over reacted in this."

"We are not here for that. There has been an autopsy carried out on Mrs Meadows and she was murdered. We are here investigating a murder Mr Nightingale."

He looked shocked. "You can't think I had something to do with it?"

"Well you and June Pulford do seem to have had motive."

Mandy and Sam watched his departure before speaking. "Well that is a man that seems quite capable of murder. We need to check his military record and his where he served but given his age he could well have seen action ," said Mandy.

"Did you believe his explanation as to what he was doing in her room. I mean he could easily have been planting the poison in her medication or the vitamins that her daughter supplied."

"Or her daughter could have just popped the odd poison pill in the vitamins," said Mandy

"Or  Elvira Mercado could have. Don't forget twenty thousand is a lot if you are trying to support you family in the Philippines."

"The person of most interest has to be Tina Thorndyke. She had to cover up her theft of the nearly half a million and.."

"She knew that arsenic had been used to poison Sybil Meadows and we had not revealed that to her," said Sam.

# Chapter 11

June Pulford sat quietly waiting for Mandy to speak. She had seen Tina and John enter the room earlier. Mandy had allowed little time for any discussion to take place between them. She hoped that this would allow each to give an independent perspective when questioned.

"I would like to know about your relationship with Sybil Meadows?" said Mandy.

"Is it true that she was poisoned?"

"I am afraid so," came the reply.

"I don't understand. Was it food poisoning or something?"

"It was definitely the, or something," said Sam somewhat sarcastically.

"Would you be so kind as to answer my question," persisted Mandy while giving Sam a look of rebuke. He shrugged.

"What was the question?"

Mandy was trying to decide if June was distracted or deliberately playing to her age and stereotype. "I should like to know about you and Sybil, how did you get on, did you like her and if you can think of any reason why anyone would want to harm her?"

"We were friends. We naturally gravitated to each other. We had a lot in common."

"And yet you almost came to blows?" said Sam.

"That was nothing, a tiff."

"What was it about?"

There was a pause as June seemed to think how to put matters in the best light. She had clearly made her decision and began to speak. "It was over John, Mr Nightingale if the truth be known. John and I had sort of struck up an affinity, a sort bond of friendship. She was getting less of my attention and she was put out."

"That is not quite how we heard it." said Sam.

"What the room incident?" Mandy nodded. June continued. "It was something in nothing. John was trying to ease the tension, placate her really. We all live cheek by jowl here so it is easier if there isn't tension or bad feelings. It makes it miserable for everyone If there are petty squabbles."

June carried on talking. "Anyway John thought that he ought to do something to make things better between Sybil and me. He saw that she had run out of her favourite perfume and because she couldn't get to the shops owing to the coronavirus lock down he thought he would buy her a bottle."

"How did he buy it?" said Mandy.

"I don't know. I suppose on the inter net? Anyway he thought he would surprise her by replacing the almost empty bottle in her room. Then it just backfired. She came back, found him in her room and all hell broke loose."

"And you decided to have it out with her?"

"No it was not about that directly. She had it in her head that John was praying on me. It was ridiculous really, She implied that he was just using me and that I was being taken advantage of. It was nonsense she was jealous I think."

"Yet as I understand, it you have funded his stay at High View?"

"Well that's not how it is. It's the coronavirus. He is just waiting for the money to come through from the sale of his flat. It is a loan until he can get himself straight."

"And yet Sybil saw it differently?"

"She was biased. After she found him in her room she became fixated with him. She said he had taken something from her room and she was going to get to the bottom of it. She said she would prove he was just out to take advantage of me. That's what sparked the flair up really. I am a grown woman. Much as Sybil and I were friends she had no right to interfere in my life. I told her so in plain English."

"I see," said Mandy. "Can I ask how you came to meet John. I mean you seem to have know him for a very short time."

"At our age time is something you don't have a great deal of. You have to make the most of what you have left. I met John in Eastbourne, on the pier. I spilt an ice cream over him. I helped clean him up and we went for afternoon tea in the tearooms on the pier. After that we met up and things went from there."

"Who suggested he reallocated to High View?"

There was a pause while she thought. "I really couldn't say. It just came about and seemed to make sense."

"One last question. Can you think or any reason why anyone would want to murder Sybil?"

"I didn't and I certainly can't think of why anyone else would."

They watched her leave the room. "What do you think," said Mandy as they waited for Elvira Mercado to arrive.

"I don't really know what to make of it. We obviously need to check out this Nightingale fellow. To me he just sounds like a con merchant and that Sybil had his number. Then there's this doctor and the fake Will, he had a good motive."

"The Will is just too rubbish a forgery for anyone to take it seriously. He is far too intelligent to think that it would pass muster," said Mandy.

"Well then there has to be a reason why some one would fake the Will and point the finger at him. Don't forget he did cover up the cause of death on the certificate."

"It could have been an oversight, a genuine mistake, or just plain laziness and incompetence. More to the point who would benefit from her death, certainly not Dr Passmore?"

"The obvious candidate is Tina Thorndyke she had her fingers in Sybil's pocket to the tune of nearly half a million quid."

"She claims it was an investment and we have no real evidence to say it was not. She claims the paper work was delayed again due to this lock down. Of course if she's lying then she had a good motive for wanting her out of the way."

"Still leaves the question as to why Dr Passmore would cover it up with a fake death certificate?" said Sam.

"Then there's the daughter, Stephenie. She was being cut of from the money and her husband is in financial trouble. Don't forget she could easily have poisoned her with the vitamin pills."

"Well anyone of them had the opportunity to poisoned her," said Sam.

Elvira Mercado knocked and entered the room interrupting the discussion. Under his breath Sam muttered "and here's another suspect with a motive."

# Chapter 12

As Elvira Mercado settled herself in the chair opposite Mandy and Sam there was a knock at the door. A figure entered dressed in the white protective suiting of the police forensics team with the addition of a protective face mask and eye shield. "We have finished up in Mrs Meadows suite," said the somewhat indistinct female voice from within the layers of protective clothing.

"Anything of note?" said Mandy.

"We have taken fingerprints and anything that could or might have contained poison along with other objects that may have been handled. We will test the prints and exclude those who we know to have a legitimate right to be in her room, nurse, cleaners and the like. We shall test for DNA and try and match up, exclude the legitimate and see what we are left with."

"How will you take samples?" said Sam.

"We don't want to be spreading the virus and become a source of infection so have set up in the garden and we shall get each of the residents to take a swab themselves for the DNA. We will disinfect the finger print scanner after each scan."

"Seems a plan, go to it," said Mandy.

The door closed and Mandy turned her attention back to Elvira Mercado. "Sorry about that, now I understand that you built up a sort of friendship with Mrs Meadows?"

"Is it true what they are saying? Was she murdered?"

"I am afraid so.."

"Oh Lord that is , that is .." she faltered for words. Sam and Mandy could see that she appeared to be genuinely shaken by the news.

"As I was saying," Mandy pushed to get the interview back on track, "tell me about Mrs Meadows?"

Elvira composed herself. "She was a nice lady. Always kind and thoughtful to me. I cannot believe someone would harm her."

"We are getting a slightly different picture of her," said Sam. "Did she not fall out with Mr Nightingale and Mrs Pulford? We heard that it almost came to blows?"

"There is something not right about that man, she knew he is not a good man."

"What makes you think that?" said Mandy.

"I see men like him all the time. They use people. They only pretend to be nice but they have other reasons. He is such a man."

"Do you have any reason though other than your feelings?"

"I hear things and I see things."

"Yes but specifically?" said Sam.

"Well he asked me to let him in her room."

"To leave a present, some perfume she had run out of due to the lock down caused by the pandemic, surely?" said Mandy.

"That's what he said."

"I don't really understand. If you thought he was up to no good why did you let him in?"

"Well at the time I didn't but...."

"But when Mrs Meadows accused him of stealing you changed your mind?"

"Well yes I had been wrong about him. I made a mistake."

"I see," said Sam. "You liked him but when Mrs Meadows fell out with him you didn't like him any more." Sam was clearly becoming annoyed by her fickleness.

"Do you know what Mr Nightingale took from her room?" Mandy attempted to salvage something of use from the interview.

"No, I am don't think he actually took anything but he seemed to go through her belongings. She said he had moved things about."

"What about Joan Pulford she introduced him to High View. How did she get on with Mrs meadows?"

"There were very close then he appeared and then they started to argue. Mrs Meadows thought he was after her money that was the top and bottom of it."

"What did you think?"

"At first I thought he was a nice man and he was making her happy. Then I started to agree with Sybil."

"So essentially you liked him, thought he was decent chap until Mrs Meadows said the contrary. At that point you had a change of heart. I wonder if that had more to do with the fact that you wanted to keep on her good side? After all she was set to leave you a sizeable sum in her Will and you wouldn't want to upset that, would you by contradicting her?" said Sam.

Elvira Mercado seemed taken aback at Sam's frankness but it was clear that he was pretty close to the mark.

Mandy followed up. "You knew then that you were to get twenty thousand pounds when she died. In fact you had access to her room and you had a motive. More to the point you now have a pretty good reason to change your opinion of John Nightingale. It would move suspicion from you to him."

"I did not kill Sybil. You should ask Tina Thorndyke and that doctor friend of hers, not me?"

"Why would you say that?"

"They're always talking. There is something going on there."

"They have to talk they have a responsibility to care for the patients."

"No, not that kind of talking. They have something going on. I think they are lovers. I have seen them kissing."

"I see. Have you overheard anything or seen anything else.?"

She was silent. Mandy felt that there was more to be told but Elvira was not to be forthcoming. "Did you know anything about a new Will?" She and Sam watched her for any reaction.

She replied, "nothing." It was clear that she would make a very poor poker player. It was clear to the two detectives that she did by her face.

"You speak very good English have you been in the UK long?" said Sam.

"English is an official language of the Philippines. I was lucky to get a good education before things got bad. My parents were in the Civil Service but then there was a new President and things changed for us. I came here to work and send money home."

They waited until she had left before speaking. "That was a waste of time," said Sam.

"I don't think it was. She told us three things. Firstly John Nightingale wasn't a petty thief. She confirmed that there is more to Thorndyke and Dr Passmore than just a professional relationship."

"And the third?" said Sam.

"The so called Will that apparently left everything to Dr Passmore, which appeared at the station, she knew of its existence."

# Chapter 13

Sam and Mandy made their way back to the car. They had left the forensics team to carry out a thorough search of High View. It would take longer than usual as social distances needed to be observed. Every room in the building needed searching including all the residents' apartments. They were mindful of not potentially spreading the virus around so a great deal of disinfecting and protective cloths changing was involved. Specifically they were looking for anyone having arsenic.

Mandy sat in the passenger seat while Sam remained on the pavement fumbling through his pockets. "What the matter?" she asked.

"Pen," he replied.

"There are lots of pens at the station. Let's go."

"No my pen, the pen my wife gave men so I wouldn't keep losing them and having to look for one. I've lost it."

"That makes no sense."

"It does to my wife. She gave me an expensive pen for our wedding anniversary. She said that way I would have to look after it because if I lost it I was a dead man."

"And you lost it?"

"I must have left it back at the Home." He turned and headed back towards the door. He realised that to enter he needed to take precautions and would need to redress in a forensics suite before wandering around a building full of elderly, high risk individuals.

He thought about the situation. There was no way he could lose the pen. He started scrolling through his mobile phone. He pressed dial. The forensics officer inside the building eventually answered. Sam explained to her that his pen was probably still on the desk where they had carried out the interviews. While she went to retrieve the pen and bring it to him, he walked round the building to wait in the garden.

Rounding the corner he saw two figures talking in the shadow of the trees. Intuition or years of experience whatever the reason he decided to not make his presence know. He recognised John Nightingale and a young man deep in conversation. He could only make out the odd word.

John said, "did you get it?"The reply was unclear but Sam thought he heard something about the usual place. The meeting broke up and the young man headed towards a small out building at the bottom of the garden while John Nightingale entered the main building by a small side door that in the past Sam assumed had been used a the tradesman's entrance.

When he was sure that Nightingale was out of sight Sam walked down the garden. It was clear as he passed the hedge that screened the bottom of the garden from view of the main building he saw the sheds and greenhouses. It was clear that this was where the pots, lawn mowers and other gardening equipment was stored. The young man was settling down into a deck chair and in the process of lighting a hand rolled cigarette as Sam rounded the hedge.

"You do know cannabis is illegal don't you?" The young man leapt to his feet and looked like he was about to have a heart attack. "DS Sam Shaw," he produced his warrant card and waved it vaguely in the man's direction.

"Look, it is only personal use," he said quickly extinguishing the joint.

"I am not that interested in the cannabis but I am interested in what you are doing with Mr Nightingale. I should say that if you muck be about I could easily change my interest."

"We have a sort of arrangement." He began to relax realising that he was not about to be nicked and lose his job.

"Go on," urged Sam.

"It's the lock down really. The residents are trapped in the Home. It means they can't get out to do their usual. Mr Nightingale likes a gamble, a smoke and a drink. I get him fags and some booze."

"Surely they can get a drink in High View?"

"They won't go against the medical advice. If the doc says, so and so shouldn't have booze then they won't sell it to them. It's something to do with liability or duty of care. I think its a load of old rubbish. I mean they may be old but it's up to them if they want to go on the lash."

"So you get them drink and tobacco?" Sam looked at the plants under glass. He noted the elaborate lighting system. "And that isn't cannabis growing there I suppose?"

He was silent for a moment. "They get aches and pains. It easy them. What's the harm?"

"Ignoring the fact that you are growing cannabis with intent to supply from your point of view I suppose none. From my point of view you are a drug dealer."

"Hold on it is just a few plants. I grew them for personal use and I just help out the old buffers now and again."

"And make yourself a few bob in the process. What's your name?"

"Thomas, Tom Welbeck"

"And pray tell where do you live?"

"Here, " came the reply.

"What in the shed?"

Tom stood up and Sam followed him into the brick built outhouse. He opened the door. Inside the once upon a time store had been converted into an almost luxurious abode. Tom had a small shower, sink, cooker, sofa bed, television and laptop on a small folding table. It was cramped but perfectly habitable. Sam was impressed. "you did this."

"It already had water, electric and drainage. It was a workshop come potting shed in the past. So everything was here. It was just a matter of scrounging together a few bits. No one ever comes down here. Tina Thorndyke only pays the bare minimum and I was struggling to pay rent on my flat so I though what the hell."

"Do you have a toilet?"

"There is the old outside privy. It is gross but some caustic soda and a bit of elbow grease and it serves the purpose. I only need it at night. In the day time I have access to the loo in the main building."

"I have one more question. Have you been asked to buy anything from the chemists for the residents?"

"Like drugs you mean?"

"I mean anything?"

"Mr Nightingale asked me to buy some perfume once apart the usual from fags and booze that's about it."

Sam began walking away to retrieve his pen from the front steps where it had been left. "Get rid of the plants. I'll be back to check." he said as a parting shot.

# Chapter 14

Mandy had the team gathered in the incident room. Social distancing observed, she started her briefing. "Salient points so far for those that have been working at home and may not be up to speed," she began to list. "We received a communication, anonymously that Mrs Sybil Meadows had been murdered at High View residential home. Sam and I visited the establishment and having spoken to the manager we were more or less satisfied that the death was natural. Then a a copy of her Will arrived here, again from an anonymous source. It had been recently drawn up and left all the deceased assets to her doctor. The same doctor who had certified her death as natural, Dr Passmore. It should be said that even a cursory glance at the Will would reveal it as a forgery."

She continued. "We interviewed her solicitor, a Mr Harwood. He revelled a number of interesting facts. Tina Thorndyke had received a substantial sum recently, around four hundred and fifty thousand pounds which she claimed was an investment in High View. We have seen no paper work to support that claim."

"A nurse, come career, Elvira Mercado also benefited from her death to the tune of twenty thousand pounds. These raised sufficient suspicion surrounding the death that we obtained the go ahead for an autopsy."

"The other beneficiaries of her death are her daughter and husband Stephenie and Jeffrey Foster and her husband's son from his previous marriage, Matthew Meadows. Now Sam has the full results of the autopsy and will share them with us. He will then hand out the areas to be investigated and task each of you."

Sam stood. "Right as we all know Mrs Sybil Meadows was murdered by arsenic poisoning. The problem as we all know with a poisoning is that you don't have to be near the victim at the time of the murder. The poison can be left in a drink, put in food or anything really the intended victim may consume at some stage. This effectively rules out the usual sources of evidence as to placing a murderer at the scene, so figure prints or DNA are of little help either."

"That leaves us with motive. To be fair there seems to be a fair amount of that around and the cause of death, the arsenic. DI Pile and I initially interviewed the doctor, Passmore as he was the obvious person with the access to drugs and on the face of it motive. He denies falsifying the cause of death and any knowledge of the so called Will. It is impossible to contradict the medical opinion as it is exactly that, an opinion. The fact that he was rubbish at determining the cause of death or did it deliberately is not something we can get anywhere with."

Mandy interrupted. "I should say that there does seem to be more than a professional relationship between the good doctor and the owner of the Home, Tina Thorndyke. Now whether he would lie on the death certificate to cover for her is a matter of conjecture. She could of course have easily poisoned the victim, on her own or perhaps helped by Dr Passmore."

Sam continued. "Turning to the lab report and assigning tasks, the cause of death is arsenic poisoning. A lethal amount of over a thousand micro grammes was administered. Merryweather I need you to figure out how you get your hands on arsenic in this day and age and if anyone on the list of suspects did so."

Potts spoke. "I know that it is used in chemotherapy for leukaemia. I had a relative who had it."

Siskin added to the conversation, "weed killer and fly paper."

"I think they banned its use donkeys years ago," said Mandy.

"I'll check. You would be surprised what you can buy on the internet," said Merryweather.

"Continuing," said Sam. "We also know that Sybil had a falling out with John Nightingale and June Pulford, both residents. And last and not least there is a young bloke living in the potting shed that grows weed and acts as a gofer for some of the residents."

"So let's start digging," said Mandy as Sam handed out each DCs assignment. Potts and Siskin were set to digging up as much background information on Elvira Mercado, Stephenie and Jeffrey Foster, the stepson Matthew Meadows, Tina Thorndyke, Thomas Passmore, John

Nightingale and June Pulford. "We need to know about our victim and her relationship with these people."

"As I see it this Tina and her doctor friend are the obvious candidates. She has been nicking the victim's money and is probably going to be exposed. The doctor has access to the drugs and can cover up the death." Said Siskin.

"It is the most likely. I admit," said Mandy. "However it doesn't explain the Will. You would have to be pretty stupid to commit a murder and then put yourself in the frame with such an obvious forgery."

"But the cause of death. It is hard to believe he could miss arsenic," pushed Siskin.

Sam said. "He could have just made a mistake or perhaps he thought Tina had poisoned her and covered up for her after the event."

"Or, we could keep open minds and investigate the facts before trapping ourselves in a single scenario. Find out everything about the people in her life. Find out who actually had access to the arsenic. Find out how it got into our victim. In fact let's do what it says on our job description be detectives rather than theorists," said Mandy.

# Chapter 15

The sun was out and there was no rain. It had not rained for over a month. Stephenie and Jeffrey Foster's garden reflected the lack of water. The lawn was yellow and bald patches were appearing in the grass. Mandy and Sam sat two metres from the Fosters on garden chairs while their children played at the end of the garden.

"Do they go back soon?" Mandy indicated the children with a glance in their direction.

"School is open for the infants but it will be some while before these two go back. So how can we help?"

Mandy was mindful that she had just suffered the loss of her mother. "I have to give you my condolences on your recent loss. I know this is a very upsetting time but given the circumstances we need to gather as much information as possible as quickly as possible. I hope you understand?"

"We know and it is hard to believe. Who would want to kill Sybil? It doesn't make any sense?" said Jeffrey.

"That is what we are trying to find out. We need your and your wife's cooperation," said Sam.

"Please think. Can you think of any reason as to why anyone would want your mother dead?" Mandy followed up.

Tears formed in Stephenie's eyes. "It sounds so brutal hearing it spoken like that in the cold light of day. It is impossible to imagine who would do such a thing. I can't get my head around it. Are you sure it was deliberate? Could it not have been an accident? It just doesn't seem to be real."

"I am sorry but the autopsy points to poisoning. The fact that it was arsenic really does put it beyond doubt that it was deliberate. So please think. What reason could anyone want for your mother's death?"

There was silence. It was clear that Stephenie was struggling to come up with a motive. Her husband intervened. "I don't think we know of anyone who would wish her harm."

"There was that silly argument with that woman June and that chap John. I think it was a storm in a tea cup. Don't forget these people are isolated with the lock down and they are in each others faces day in and day out. There are bound to be disagreements. I can't really see June or John as murders though."

"Do you know the details?"

"Not really, you have to bear in mind that I haven't had a chance to really talk with mum.." her voiced trailed off and she muffled a sob. "I won't ever get the chance now to talk again. I won't ever be able to tell her I love her." Mandy and Sam sat silently waiting as she controlled her grief. Her husband put his arms round her and made consoling noises. The sobbing had attracted the children's attention and they were looking anxiously at their mother. They were two girls about eight and ten years old.

"Mummy is fine. She is just sad about grandma," said Jeffrey to the children. They hesitated briefly before resuming their play.

"June Pulford and John Nightingale," prompted Sam.

Stephenie regained her composure. "Mum though he had been in her room, going through her stuff. They didn't get on. Mum had it in her head that he was just after June's money."

"What did you think?"

"I thought it was nonsense. To my mind they just wanted a bit of company in their old age but there was no convincing Mum."

Jeffrey said. "Sybil just took an instant dislike to the man. She said he was a bad lot and she would prove it. I think she was a bit jealous at him coming between June and her."

At that point his wife intervened. "You make Mum sound horrible, possessive. She was not like that at all. She was just concerned for her friend. She didn't want her to get hurt."

"Did she say if anything had been taken from her room?"

"It was anything like that. John had persuaded that carer, what's her name, Elvira to let him in her room. To my mind you would have to be the worst thief ever if you went and got someone to let you in. He had a perfectly simple explanation in that he had obtained her favourite perfume and wanted to surprise her. It was an attempt to mend the divide between her, him and June." Said Jeffrey.

Stephenie clearly did not agree with her husband. "She was adamant that he had been rummaging through her things."

"Was she specific?"

"Her photograph albums had been moved. She thought he was somehow checking up on her.."

"Or just a fastidious cleaner," Jeffrey added.

"I see," said Mandy. "We need to examine motive. We have spoken to her solicitor and it is clear that you and your husband benefit the most from her death. We understand that you are struggling financially?"

"Who told you that?" Jeffrey was clearly angered by the suggestion.

Looking at Stephenie, Mandy continued. "You were overheard arguing with your mother. She made it clear in no uncertain terns that she was unwilling to advance anyone money to put into Jeffrey's business. How is your business Mr Foster?"

Jeffrey was red faced, seething with anger and barely controlling his temper as he replied. "She was being stubborn and short-sighted. It was a great investment opportunity. The business is doing really well."

Sam raised an eyebrow. "We will check, you know."

"Stop it," Stephenie clearly was at breaking point. "Stop it Jeffrey the business is a disaster and the pandemic has finally put it out of its misery. The only reason we have managed so far is on handouts from my Mum. You have to face reality at some stage, It has to stop."

It was self evident that all was not sweetness and light in the Foster household. The was silence as realisation dawned on the couple that they had demonstrated clear motive for wanting Sybil dead.

Sam as insensitive as usual ploughed on."Well, I think that covers the motive. So let's have a look at opportunity shall we? Mrs Thorndyke said you supplied her with vitamin tablets?"

"I worry that she wasn't getting a balanced diet. The food is good at High view but it reflects more fine dinning than nutritional excellence. I like to make sure she gets a good balanced approach."

"So you give her supplements? You do see where we are going with this?"

"You think that I poisoned my own mother?" she said.

"We need to explore every avenue and exclude wherever possible. Tell me do either of you have a medical, pharmaceutical or industrial background that would allow access to arsenic?"Sam was straight to the point.

There was a moments hesitation. Jeffrey replied first. "I was in the army and trained as a paramedic but I assure you I haven't been directly involved in anyway since. My wife did chemistry an University but went into office administration. So in answer to your question is we do not have a stash of arsenic that we use to go round murdering people."

The atmosphere had clearly deteriorated and Mandy decided nothing more was to be gained by continuing. "I understand you have a step brother, Matthew from you father's first marriage. Do you have any information as to his whereabouts?"

"I really don't know anything about him other than his name. Neither my mother nor I had any contact. I am not even sure he is even alive. I think he was in Africa or somewhere."

"Do you know anything about his mother, your fathers first wife?"

"Nothing I am sorry. He and Mum never spoke of it."

# Chapter 16

Driving to Dr Thomas Passmore's surgery Mandy was in a reflective mood. Sam had as usual taken the wheel. She always let him drive prompting him to come up with the now running joke that she never drove because she was so posh she had always had a chauffeur. At one stage she had obtained a old style flat policeman's cap from the property office and placed it on the drivers seat. He rose to the occasion, put the cap on and circled the car and opened the door for her, proclaiming "your limousine awaits your highness."

"I have serious doubts as to if we will make any headway with this case. I just cannot see how we will be able to prove it even if we can solve who actually committed the crime. We are knee deep in motives and suspects. It is a poisoning though and so there is no definite time. We can't say when it was introduced and how."

"Well at least we know Sybil never left High View so the poison had to have been brought in. So realistically we have to link the poison to a person."

"The difficulty in obtaining arsenic is the saving grace. Dr Passmore seems to be the obvious candidate. With hospital appointments suspended he may well be administering arsenic based  chemotherapy to some cancer patients."

She rummaged in her bag and pulled out a sheet of paper. It was some notes Potts had prepared. "There is a drug called Trisenox used to treat," she paused formulating the pronunciation. " a type of acute myeloid leukaemia called acute promyelocyte leukaemia. I am not sure what that is exactly but it seems it can be given orally or injected at home by a medical professional."

"So we need to see if our doctor was treating anyone with it."

"That won't be easy. We can ask and get information on Sybil Meadows but we cannot just ask to rummage through his patients records to see who and what they are being treated for. No judge would grant us a warrant to do so either. He could have enough arsenic in one form or another to sink the titanic and we have no way of finding out."

"However he is the most likely candidate by a long shot, medically qualified, access to the deceased and access to the drugs."

"You say that but we have enough candidates with medical training and the necessary access to our victim. Jeffrey Foster had medical training in the army. Both Tina Thorndyke and Elvira Mercado have a nursing backgrounds. We know nothing yet about June Pulford or John Nightingale."

"On the other hand John and June have no motive. The big winners here are Tina, Elvira, Stephenie and her husband Jeffrey. All were desperate for money."

"Don't forget her step son, her husband's boy from his first marriage, Michael. We don't even know where he is or if he is still alive. We need a lot more information. Hopefully when we get back to the station Potts, Merryweather and Siskin will have made some progress looking into all their backgrounds."

They arrived at the surgery. It felt very strange as they made their way to the building. Normally the waiting area would be packed with patients waiting to be seen by the doctors. There would be postnatal clinics, holiday vaccination, blood and ECG tests all be carried out by the practice nurses. Today there was no one. Patients entered one at a time and wore masks. Some who had arrived early for their appointments were waiting, two metres apart outside. Mandy and Sam checked the time. They donned face masks and entered.

In Dr Passmore's office they sat, with the required social distance being observed Mandy spoke. " Since we last spoke via Skype we have had the autopsy and toxicology report back. It is clear that Mrs Meadows was poisoned by arsenic." She waited for his reaction.

He showed no sign of surprise. He would have known that once an autopsy was to be carried out that the true cause of death would be exposed. "I see. It would appear that I made a mistake as to the cause of death."

"Do you have any idea how arsenic came to be in her system?"

"No idea, it certainly had nothing to do with the medication she was on. I was treating her for hypertension, high blood pressure."

"Do you have access to arsenic in one form or another."

"I specialise in elderly care, private elderly care. I only come to the practice here on rare occasions. My work as I said is solely private but with these exceptional times I have decided to devote at least part of my time to the National Health Service and do my bit. However there are a number of patients who require chemotherapy. Normally this would be administered at the hospital as day patients. With the lock down it is of course safer to administer at home. There is a drug that had proved successful in treating a specific cancer called Trisenox. It is also marketed under other names but it is an arsenic based compound."

"And you have been administering it to certain, patients?"

"Yes," he said no more.

"Are you treating anyone at High View with this drug?" said Sam bluntly.

"You know I am not able to discuss specific patients details."

"Not specific, I repeat are you treating anyone with arsenic at High View," Sam persisted.

There was a pause while the doctor considered his rely. "That day I had two patients to treat with Trisenox, neither at High View."

"Is that a low number or a great number in a day?"

"An usual state of affairs. A unique situation caused by the need for a number of colleagues to self isolate. They are unable to interact with their elderly patients, so I was lending a hand. As I said I specialise in elderly care."

"You were at High View when the argument developed between Sybil and June?" said Mandy.

"I was having a look at a minor injury to Mr Nightingale, when it kicked off, yes."

"Did you have arsenic with you?"

"I believe so, in my medical bag."

"And did you keep it in your possession at all times?"

A look of realisation passed across the doctors face. Mandy spoke, "I assume from your reaction the answer is no. So tell me who could have gained access to it?"

"I left the bag in Tina Thorndyke's office, the door was open, so anyone could have had access, I suppose but I did not miss any of the doses."

"Can you be sure?"

From he expression it  was clear again that the answer was going to be no. "I was in a hurry, running late. The batches had been delivered to my private practice from my colleagues and I just grabbed a handful. I never bothered to check."

"Not looking good is it, wrong cause of death, failure to properly track medications?"

He said nothing, Sam did, "And there is still the matter of a badly forged Will naming you as the sole beneficiary."

# Chapter 17

1993 Johannesburg night air was filled with the sound of buzzing insects. Gunner Jack stood in the shadows smoking a cigarette. He had been watching the house for over two hours. It had taken him over two years to get to this point. He had suspected nothing. It had come as a complete shock and his whole life had disintegrated in that one instant just under two years ago.

He had been up country away for ten days. He had arrived back. His son and the nanny were there. "Where's Elenor? Is she due back soon?" He asked the nanny.

"The mistress left to visit her mother the day after you left."

"Her mother is dead," he said. The nanny looked bemused. "My son?" he asked.

"In bed," he rushed to the nursery his three old son was sleeping soundly.

Elenor never came back. Over the next few days he found out that his partner Patrick Meadows had disappeared leaving his wife, Shirley and son Michael. He also found out that Patrick had taken every last penny from their business and the diamonds. It ran into millions. Money was deposited in Shirley's bank account each month. It was the only descent thing Patrick did.

Gunner struggled on supporting his son and trying to find his wife and ex business partner. After two years of searching it had brought him to this point. Behind the doors and windows just yards away was the woman who had betrayed him and the man that had taken everything.

He still hesitated. The initial anger had subsided but the pain remained. It was odd. Now that he had found them his anger seemed to evaporate. He did not so much want revenge he wanted an explanation. He wanted to understand. He also wanted his money. He wanted at least that. His young son deserved better than the hand to mouth existence they now had.

The house Patrick and Elenor was more a mansion. The cars in the drive testified to their luxurious lifestyle. He and their son lived in a tiny flat struggling daily to meet the bills. He could not understand how Elenor could just abandon them, abandon her son but she had. She just had that bit of her humanity missing. She had never wanted to be a mother. There were just some people like that. The lacked the instinct most have.

He and Patrick had left the army and set up in security. The conflict in Sierra Leone was hotting up and diamonds were funding the conflict. Within in weeks of arriving in Africa they found themselves involved in the diamond trade. Selling and transporting blood diamonds as they became known for the RUF, the rebel faction. They were rich almost overnight. It was a case of right place, right time and the right skill set.

Then it all came crashing down for gunner. His wife and so called partner ran off taking the money. He was left high and dry with a son to support. Now he was going to get payback. He walked up the door and rang the bell. The door intercom was answered by the maid.

"I am here to see Mr Meadows. Tell him that Gunner is here."

There was a delay as she presumably consulted with the master of the house. The door eventually opened and Patrick stood in the hallway. "You found me then," he said almost nonchalantly. The interior of the house was palatial. Gunner could feel the anger and resentment rising as he followed him into the vast reception room.

Elenor stood facing them as they entered. There was a total look of disdain on her face. It was clear to Gunner that she viewed him as an irritant, a nuisance. She had discarded him, abandoned her small son and yet she regarded her husband as nothing more than a passing inconvenience in her life. As he faced her he realised that there was nothing to this woman except self interest and greed.

"Why have you come?" said Patrick.

"You stole everything from me and you have the balls to ask me that?" He addressed Elenor. "You are my wife. You have a son. Are you not a bit interested in him at least."

She looked at him as though he had appeared from another

universe. "You wanted a kid. I never did. You have one. So what's the problem? You are just pathetic. You never gave me what I wanted. I realised that Patrick was the real man. He had the guts, the drive to go after something he wanted and get it. You were always going to be the loser. I didn't want a loser."

"You heard what you needed to know. Now now piss off," said Patrick. "You were always the nice guy, even in the army."

"You stole all the money.."

"Well I stole the money that we stole in the first place. Why don't you go to the police. I am sure they will overlook your involvement in blood diamonds and the mass murder in Sierra Leone we helped fund. I'll tell you why because Elenor is right you are gutless."

Gunner did not know what he had expected coming here. He knew that neither of these two had any saving grace. He tried, "what about your son, Michael your wife? What about Shirley?"

"For crying out loud that drab sow and that bleating kid of mine. They are fine. I see them alright financially. What more can they want. You might have been happy being mister house husband but we are here only once so I am going to make sure I get it all and live it to the full. So run along and leave Elenor and me to live our lives."

To add insult to injury Elenor could not resist goading him. "You heard the real man. Now run along."

The rage built in Gunner. The anger was like a descending white mist. He began to rush at Patrick. "I shouldn't do anything stupid if I were you." A gun was in Patrick's hand. Gunner did not know where it had appeared from. He stopped.

There was silence as the two men faced off. Patrick continued. "I think you should go. There is nothing for you here. For old times sake I won't kill you but I must admit it is an option I am giving serious thought to. It would be self defence. You invaded my home and I shot you."

The next few moments would never be fully clear in Gunner's mind. Patrick may have been a self interested sociopath and had no qualms in committing murder but that did not make him good at it. Gunner despite having no innate killer instinct had proved to be exceptional at close combat and a crack marksman. A talent that had become evident when the were both in the army. The nick name Gunner was well earned.

Instinct and training kicked in. Patrick was unprepared for the speed at which Gunner closed the distance between them. In the blink of an eye the two men were locked in a life and death embrace. The gun was the prize. Patrick trying to fire it into Gunner and Gunner trying to wrest it from him.

The gun came from Patrick's grasp and as it did so the sound of the shot broke the silence of the night. Their ears rang at the retort. Then the sound of screaming filled their ears as their hearing retuned. Blood was spurting from Eleanor's neck. She slumped to her knees., then silence. Gunner stood holding the weapon as he watched her die. He was numb, stunned unmoving paralysed with shook.

Patrick saw his opportunity and rushed from the room, fleeing the house while Gunner remained just staring at his deceased wife. He slowly became aware of the shouting outside and the general commotion. Patrick was shouting, " help, murder call the police."

# Chapter 18

"I am not very happy with our doctor Passmore are you?" said Sam. They were sat in Mandy's office and Sam was, as usual spilling crumbs on her desk from a bacon sandwich.

"Here's a my biggest mystery. How come, even though there is a lock down of all restaurants do you still have a constant supply of bacon sandwiches? Do you have an underground network of illicit sandwich makers? Is there a criminal cartel that has sprung up to supply people addicted to bacon? More to the point are you the master mind behind what will become know as the Mr Pork, bacon sandwich cartel?"

Sam laughed and to Mandy's dismay more crumbs were added to the tally on her desk. "It is Bert. He has converted to a delivery service."

Mandy realised as soon as she spoke that she was going to regret asking,"Bert?"

"You know Bert. Everybody at the nick knows Bert. Bert is a legend." Mandy shook her head and her regret at ever mentioning the crumbs increased by the moment. "Bert was a criminal, very minor, flogging stolen lead, a bit of pickpocketing, passing the odd dud fiver, that sort of thing. Even he realised that he wasn't very good at it. Anyway the desk sergeant here, Wilkins getting fed up with booking him so suggested he should go straight. In the ensuing discussion, bearing in mind this was the time they were downsizing the nick, closing the canteen and just putting in the vending machines, the lack of catering came up. The rest is history, Bert went straight, his Cafe was borne and the coppers here had bacon sarnies twenty four seven. If we had an all nighter Bert could be relied on to come in, open up and cook egg and chips at two or three in the morning."

Mandy realised she had dug herself a hole but found she was intrigued and could not throw away the shovel. Digging herself deeper, "I haven't seen a Bert's Cafe."

"That's because Bert retried about two years ago."

"I know I am going to regret asking but how come there is what remains of a bacon sandwich scattered across my desk?"

"Well, Bert as a one time career criminal appreciated the workings of the boys in blue. He realised that with all the usual eateries shut there was a unsatisfied demand. He contacted the nick, the custody officer takes the orders and the nosh appears. Everyone is happy," said Sam.

"How come no one asks for my order?"

Sam was hesitant. "I am not judging, I mean each to his own and all that but.."

"But what?"

"Bert is old school, bacon, egg and extra grease. He doesn't do avocado and falafel. I am not even sure if he knows what a lettuce is. You are a vegetarian and we didn't want to upset you."

"Right I see. It would have been nice to have been asked," she muttered.

"Dr Passmore," said Sam making a feeble attempt to pick up the crumbs on her desk but only succeeding in brushing them across the floor.

"I don't have him down for it. I think he is obviously involved with Tina Thorndyke. I think he thought she had something to do with the poisoning and out of missed placed loyalty just didn't dig too deeply. He just signed it off a natural death. In the midst of a pandemic he just assumed no one would give an elderly person's death a second look."

"True and he has not actually committed a crime that can be proved. At most he would get a rap over the knuckles from the Medical council for being careless. There wouldn't be a GP left in the Country if they were all struck off for making mistakes in diagnosing."

"The arsenic is more troubling though. We can safely assume that he is not the most diligent of personalities and is fairly casual in his methods. He doesn't do much real doctoring and focusses on looking after the old and wealthy, pandering to them and charging a fortune for doing so. All of a sudden he finds himself administering this Trisenox to elderly patients who can't attend the hospitals owing to the virus."

"He carries it around in his bag which he appears to just leave lying around. You are right. It doesn't help us but anyone could have got hold of the stuff and it seems he would be little the wiser."

"It strikes me that even if he knew arsenic had gone from his bag he probably wouldn't say anything. He virtually admitted to us that he left the bag unattended when he administered to John Nightingale."

"Tina had to be our obvious choice of suspect. She gets him to leave his bag and send him off to see Nightingale. She then has a quick rummage through his medical bag. Spots Trisenox and knows that it is lethal from all her years in the profession. Anyway the packaging is covered in warnings as to its toxicity."

"That's the problem though anyone looking through the bag would spot it as a good bet to poison someone with, So it does not really narrow it down much."

They sat thinking for a moment. "Let's see what Potts, Siskin and Merryweather have found out so far. They left the office and called for attention.

"Any one got anything on the poison?" said Sam.

Siskin spoke first. "The detail is in. The source of the arsenic was Trisenox. It was probably administered orally. They have been unable to analyse the exact compound so we they can't tell us the exact origin."

"In other words we can't say it was a match to Dr Passmore's," said Mandy.

"Well where else would it have come from?" said Sam.

Potts interjected. "The internet."

"What do you mean?" said Mandy somewhat surprised.

"You can buy it on line. Most of it comes from India. Click on the dose the type and you get it through the post."

"You are kidding? There must be controls, surely?"

"There are in theory but it took me a couple of minutes to get through them. Anyone with a bit of savvy could get a delivery." Potts pointed to the parcel on his desk. "Enough to teat a half a dozen patients or kill all the coppers in the nick."

"Of that is just great," said Sam. "That complicates matters just a bit."

"It may just help," said Mandy. "Look at it this way. We were never going to be able to put the smoking gun in anyone's hand. It was always going to be down to motive. The fake Will was an attempt to push the crime onto Dr Passmore and we have no hard evidence that Tina Thorndyke had not entered into a genuine business relationship with Sybil Meadows whereby she was investing the half a million pounds."

She continued, "we need to dig deeper. Find out who really benefited from Sybil's death. Now we know that the doctor was not the only person with access to the poison we are a bit closer to finding out who killed her."

# Chapter 19

DC Merryweather had been distracted during the discussions, tapping at his computer. He finally focussed back on the conversation taking place between Mandy and the rest of his colleagues. "I have something," he spoke.

"Nice of you to join us," said Sam in his usual curmudgeonly manner. Go on then tell us."

"I have a result back for fingerprints taken from Sybil Meadows' room. We have a match, John Night. I put his picture up in the big screen." The bid screen was rather less than big it was a twenty four inch TV mounted on the wall next to the white board used to keep track of the investigation.

Nothing appeared. They waited some more, nothing appeared. "Hold on I can get this," said Merryweather.

"Or not," said Sam.

"Just print it," Mandy finally said as Merryweather continued to tap away at his keyboard. He looked disappointed but started the printer running. Siskin got up and collected the output. They finally each held the photograph of John Night.

"Well we know this guy," said Sam, "John Nightingale."

"AKA John Night, John Knight, Nigel Night and so on. What a lovely fellow," said Mandy. "Look at his form. Possession of class A drugs, fraud, petty theft it goes on and on."

"That was mostly when he was a kid. He seems to have moved on to being a con man." Sam had turned to the second page and his more recent convictions. "He is focussing on conning old ladies out of their money. Two jail terms for obtaining money by deception."

"It would appear that our Mr Nightingale has not found true love with June Pulford after all. Sybil was right then. He was up to no good and taking June for a ride."

"A bit more information," said Merryweather. "In her statement she said that he was in the process of selling his flat In Eastbourne. I am checking the land registry as we speak. His name doesn't appear on the title."

"So he doesn't own a flat, so no sale proceeds and no chance of paying June Pulford back. She is being stitched up like a kipper," said Potts.

"There is no history of violence in his criminal record though," observed Mandy. "It is a big step from conning old ladies to murder. What do you think, Sam?" said Mandy.

"I take your point. I have known a few murderers over the years. I admit that there is usually a history of escalating violence before a murder is committed. The signs are often there from an early age, anti social behaviour, mental instability such as psychosis, personality disorders and sociopathic behaviour traits. Of course that is a generalisation. A lot of murders are unintentional, in fact most are, a burglary gone wrong, an argument that ends in violence or a drink too many. No on the face of it I agree. I don't see Mr Night , Nightingale or whoever he is, as a cold blooded killer. A scumbag yes but a killer no."

"He has nerve though. He most have known that he would be found out when we swabbed for prints and yet he sat in front of us and did not bat and eyelid when we questioned him," mused Mandy.

"Well, he wouldn't be much of a con artist if he was rubbish at lying," said Siskin.

Mandy laughed, "that is a good point. We need to dig deeper though. Unlikely as it is that he has changed his modus operandi he has motive. If Sybil Meadows was threatening to expose him he stood to lose a good source of income in June Pulford. We have to keep an open mind."

"So what about the rest of the fingerprints in Sybil's room?" said Sam.

"No match to the criminal database," said Merryweather

"That's a pity. Life would be so much easier if they turned up a nice homicidal maniac. Okay keep checking and see what else you can turn up."

"The one person that seems out of the picture is this Matthew

Meadows, Patrick meadows son from his first marriage. We need to find out where he is," said Sam. "Does anyone have anything?"

"I have phoned  Mr Harwood at Trent Styles and Pilcher, the solicitor you spoke to. I asked if they had any means of contacting Matthew. It turns out it was very simple. They just write to his bank, HSBC and they will pass on any communication."

"And have they," said Mandy.

"No not yet, they are sorting the estate, probate that sort of stuff."

"It seems we need to get a court order forcing his bank to give us his address. He is a suspect in a murder so that shouldn't prove difficult," said Sam.

"I think you'll find it will be a lot harder than that. The clue is in the name of the bank. As you know it stands for Hongkong and Shanghai banking corporation. The bank in South Africa is a branch but it is controlled from Asia not the UK. So a bit of paper from a UK judge won't get us very far."

"Why is everything so complicated these days?" moaned Sam.

"Modern life," suggested Mandy. Sam scowled. "So how is this Matthew to identify himself to the solicitors, As I understand it no one has seen him since he was a kid, certainly not his half sister Stephenie and she his the only living relative?"

"Harwood told me that his mother sent the odd photo to his father, her ex-husband of Matthew as he grew up."

"Where are these pictures now?"

"I assume they are among the stuff, forensics gathered up from Sybil's room that is if she kept her husbands stuff. In any event Trent Styles and Pilcher will eventually write to the bank and when he turns up with his birth certificate they will release the funds."

"I want to see Sybil's effects as soon as forensics have finished with them," said Mandy. "Now what about her daughter Stephenie and her son in law Jeffrey, who had been digging into them?"

# Chapter 20

"Here's what we have so far," said Merryweather. "She was privately educated and graduated with a degree in chemistry. He joined the army at eighteen and was trained as a medic. He left the Army a started the business. When I say started a business he has a long line of failed companies and business ventures."

"Not a success then?" said Sam.

"You could say that. Siskin and I have checked the usual and he has a number of online betting accounts. He had a serious gambling problem. If he has a couple of bob it doesn't stay in his pocket for long. His current venture selling surplus military supplies is a complete disaster."

"Let me guess," said Mandy. "They relied on Sybil to keep them a float."

"Yep on the button, their bank account reveals money being transferred almost weekly from her mum."

"It looks like everyone had their hand in her pocket," said Sam.

"No doubt that they were in dire straights and desperate. The fraud squad have him on their radar along with Trading Standards and the Benefits fraud detection unit."

"Well it was very convenient that her mum died then," said Sam.

"It is a big jump from needing money to killing your own Mum."

"Won't be the first time kids have hurried their parents into the next world to get their hands on their money. We know that Sybil had reached the end of her patience with Jeffrey and put her foot down. We also know that her daughter was in the habit of leaving her vitamin tablets to take. It would be easy enough to pop some poison in one and sit back and wait for the money. She had a degree in chemistry and hubby had some medical training. He could even have got the arsenic through his business."

"It can't be ruled out," said Mandy. "I am less than convinced though, I have to say."

"For a little old lady the number of people that benefited form her death seems to be mounting. Every man and his dog we come across has a reason to be happy she died. Even the care worker Elvira got something out of her death," commented Potts.

"True but that does not make them murderers," said Mandy. "Let's keep to the evidence. Have we run all the fingerprints in her room through every data base and do we have any unidentified prints in her room, ones that just should not be there?"

Siskin checked the forensic report, "no the only figure prints in the room were all accounted for. They are the people you would expect to be there including our con man Night and her closest friend June Pulford."

"We seem to be hitting a brick wall. What we need is information. The clue to this is the anonymous phone call alerting us to the death and the fake Will putting Dr Passmore in the frame for it. I think the timing is important. We had the call which prompted our visit to High View. Only after the visit did the Will turn up. My question is why not just give us the Will in the first place. It was on the face of it far more compelling and more likely to get our attention than a telephone call. The police receive hundreds of calls all day long from cranks reporting everything from murders to Martians landing. Most of the time they are logged and that would be the end of it."

"That's true  After our initial visit we were pretty much satisfied there was nothing suspicious," said Sam.

"Exactly, then the Will turned up. Now that's the odd thing that doesn't fit. The inconsistencies that trouble me are. If you think someone is murdered why would you report it anonymously? Why do you not want to be identified? Could it be be fear of reprisal? Could you have been involved and have a guilty conscience?"

"I see. Fear of reprisal seems unlikely. If it was a drug related gang killing fear is a major factor but an elderly woman in a home doesn't make that a likely motive. Remorse is a possibility."

"Then why not just confess? No the Will is the key. We need to know who drafted it and why. It would never pass muster as the real thing so what was its purpose? It actuality it served only one purpose and that was to get us to actively investigate Sybil Meadows death as a murder."

"Well surely that makes sense. The anonymous caller saw that the murderer was going to get away with it and sent us more evidence to make sure her death was properly investigated," said Sam.

"The Will was an obvious fake. We confirmed that within hours by talking to the deceased solicitors. If the Will was the reason for the call the logical assumption was that the informer had the Will. So why not send the Will to us or why not say the doctor is murdering old ladies and getting them to leave their money to him? The only conclusion that can be drawn is that the person that tipped us off knew nothing of the Will when they called."

Sam, Potts, Siskin and Merryweather were all joined together by a shared look of confusion. "For crying out loud Boss stop with suspense." Merryweather broke first.

"So if the caller knew nothing of a Will then it is likely that they did not suspect Tina and the doctor of committing murder but had an entirely different suspect in mind. So here is what happened. The call is made. We turn up. We are satisfied. Our tipster knows there has been a murder and the murderer is going to get away with it."

She paused for brief and ordered her thoughts. "The other person we need to look at and understand is the murderer. They have murdered Sybil, poisoned her. Suddenly the police arrive. Bear in mind the killer has to be at High View either staff or a resident because the place is under lock down. The only exception is her daughter. Up to this point the killer thinks they are in the clear. Their victim's death has been certified as due to naturally causes, so no autopsy and no investigation. When we arrive that all goes out the window."

"What to do that is what our murderer asks? He or she knows that there is something going on with Tina and the doctor. Perhaps he or she suspects there is a an affair. I think the murderer realises at that point who has informed on him or at least has a good idea as to who they are. Perhaps he fears that the informer might reveal further evidence so what is to be done?"

"Murder the anonymous caller," suggested Siskin.

"Not a bad solution but a really bad idea if you want to get away with it," laughed Mandy. "But we have to assume for the moment that the killer is not a serial killing homicidal maniac. No the solution is to convince our caller that someone else did it."

"I follow you, " said Sam. "Our murderer produces the Will and says despite what you saw or think you know it wasn't me. Look I have gotten hold of the a draft copy of the new Will that shows Dr Passmore is the one you should be pointing at."

"Bear in mind that the killer had no way of knowing that we were happy that no foul play was involved and were closing the book on it at that point in time. In an attempt to divert our investigation away from themselves they actually caused us to take it seriously."

"It makes sense. The Will was faked by the killer after our visit to throw us off the scent."

"There our now two possibilities. One the initial anonymous caller was given the Will by the potential killer and they sent it to us or two they sent it themselves. The key is to getting to the bottom of it, is to identify who made the call tipping us off from High View in the first place."

# Chapter 21

The court room in Johannesburg was packed and the aged air conditioning added to the cloying atmosphere. It was the last day of the trial. Trevor Drew sat waiting with his defence team for the judge to enter. The verdict had been delivered and he was awaiting sentencing. The judge a woman had showed little empathy towards the accused throughout the proceedings. As a black woman growing up with apartheid where violence and abuse towards her gender was common place she had no sympathy to men that killed their wives.

The evidence given by Patrick Meadows had been damming.

Prosecutor, "please tell the Court in your own words what occurred the night Elenor Drew was killed?"

Patrick stood in the witness box looking every part the respectable businessman who had been the victim of a gross injustice. Gunner Drew on the other hand having spent months in the South African detention system had all the appearance of a desperate felon. Thin, gaunt and bruised around the face from an attack by a fellow inmate he had criminal and guilty write large across his entirety.

"Elenor and I were sitting in the living room when the front door was answered by the maid. She informed me that Mr Drew was at the door to see me. I went to greet him in the hallway and dismissed the maid."

Persecutor, "What frame of mind was Mr Drew in?"

"He was angry and very agitated."

Prosecutor, "Why was this?"

"Well obviously as you know Elenor was his wife and she had left him. He could not accept the situation that she no longer wanted him. We had moved away and tried to keep where we were now living a secret from him. Elenor was forced to even give up contact with their son due to Trevor's threats."

Persecutor, "so Mr Drew had made threats before?"

"Oh yes on numerous occasions and we took them seriously. I had served with Trevor in the UK military and I knew all to well what a volatile and dangerous individual he could be.."

Drew was incensed at the lies from the mouth of his ex business partner. He shouted, "that's not true. You're the sadistic bastard, you're a lying .."

His defence team pulled him to his seat and the Judge angered banged the bench. "Stop that, I will not tolerate it." Gradually silence descended in the court room. She took a deep breath and continued. Addressing his lawyer she said. "If you cannot control your client then I shall have him removed and he can sit out the rest of the proceedings in the cells downstairs."

The was a pause while his lawyer cautioned him. "It won't happen again. I have my client's assurance." The Judge waived the prosecutor on.

Prosecutor, "please continue. You were telling us that you feared this man and from your time together in the army you knew him to be of a dangerous and unstable nature."

"Yes that's right. Elenor lived in fear of his mood swings and his violence towards her. We became close when Trevor was away on business and things developed. My marriage had been in trouble for some time and we found comfort in each other. Things just took their natural course from there."

Prosecutor, "and you decided to move away together."

"There was no choice but he still tracked us down. There he was in our house ranting and raving. He pushed past me and into the living area where Elenor was cowering in fear."

Prosecutor, "what happened next?"

"He was ranting like a madman, incoherent. He was clearly deranged, out of control and enraged. He produced a gun and before I could do anything he had shot her and she fell to the ground."

Prosecutor, "what did you do then?"

"Well naturally my first reaction was to rush to the aid of the woman I loved. Then I realised he had not finished. I saw that I was to be next. I had no choice but to try and get away. Somehow, I don't know how I escaped from the house and found myself running down the street. I was screaming for help. The rest is confused but the police arrived and managed to take Trevor into custody."

Trevor Drew's lawyer did his best to break down Patrick Meadows testimony but he stuck to his version of events.

Defence. "why did Mrs Drew leave her son, David behind with her supposedly violent and unstable husband. He was away when you and she eloped. Why did you not take him with you? Surely she must have feared for the boys safety?"

"There was no choice. There was only a small opportunity to get away. She hoped at some stage to get custody and have him back."

Defence, "you abandoned you wife, Shirley and your small son Michael. It seems to me that neither you nor Mrs Drew had anything but your own self interest at heart.."

Judge, "that is an expression of opinion. Please stick to questioning and keep your opinions to yourself."

Defence, "I put it to you that you deliberately engineered a trip for Trevor Drew not with the sole intention of leaving with his wife but also with a view to stealing all the money from your joint business."

"Nonsense,"

Defence, "There was the equivalent of six million dollars in a joint account held by you and Mr Drew. The only was money could be transferred or moved was with both of you entering your part of the security code. You and Mrs Drew conspired to take the money. She somehow obtained knowledge of her husband's code. You sent him on a business trip and between you you emptied the account and absconded."

"There was no joint business, there was no account, there was no million dollars. It is fantasy made up by him to try and get off murdering his wife."

There was no breaking down Partick Meadows and as the money was acquired by illegal trading in diamonds being exported from Sierra Leone, Drew's lawyer had no way to produce paper work to back up the claims he was making. He turned to the night of Elenor's death.

Defence, "Can we turn to the gun. Where did that come from."

"I have already told you. He brought it with him."

Defence, " and yet traces of your DNA were found on it. Can you explain that?"

"Of course not I am not a scientist.

Defence, "is not the truth of the matter that Mr Drew never arrived with a gun but in fact you produced it with the intention of getting rid of him for good? It was your gun and the intention was to kill Mr Drew. You however underestimated his speed and agility and a struggle ensued during which his wife was accidentality shot and killed."

"I told you he arrived incensed and killed her."

The DNA evidence seemed to support Drew's version on events but the prosecution produced an expert who claimed that the amount of Meadow's DNA could have been as a result of transfer. If Meadow's touched Drew and Drew touched the gun that would account for it being present, In his opinion the majority of the DNA was Drew's and the gun shot residue found on him pointed to him firing the gun.

Mandy looked up from reading the transcript of the trial. "Not the nicest of fellows Sybil's husband was he?" she said to Sam who sat opposite.

"I don't see how this gets us any further," said Sam.

"Drew got life, its says here. Check out what happened to him. Is he still banged up? What happened to his and Elenor's son," she paused skipping through the paper work. "Ah, here's his name David. What happened to David Drew? Where is he now?"

"What reason could either he or his son have to harm Sybil? I accept that Patrick Meadows most likely got his wealth dealing in blood diamonds with Trevor Drew, probably smuggling them out for the Warlords in Sierra Leone. I also think that he stole the money they made from Drew but what motive could there be to murder Patrick's widow? Drew nor his kid benefit financially and as Patrick Meadows is dead he is not in a position to be upset by his wife's death emotionally, is he?"

"I agreer with what you say but there is something that tells me the answer to the Sybil Meadows murder lies is the past."

# Chapter 22

The drive to High View was uninterrupted by any other traffic on the road. Despite the partial easing of the coronavirus lock down Eastbourne remained unchanged. The predominantly elderly, retired population were taking few chances. They were the in the high risk of dying group and they were well aware of it. There was no rush back to normal life here. Eastbourne was often jokingly referred to as God's Waiting Room owing to its popularity with retirees. They were determined not to have it renamed the Fast Track to Heaven.

Sam was behind the wheel. "This car smells," Mandy commented.

"Of bacon, if you want your care to smell what better?"

"Spring flowers, pine needles or freshly baked bread," she suggested.

Sam feigned disbelief. "I don't like the sound of any of that. I have two rules in life and they have served me well. One never trust a man that wears brown shoes with a suit and two, avoid anyone who hugs trees."

"There is no logic in that at all," she laughed.

"Mock me at your peril. Every serial killer I have nicked wore brown shoes or was a vegan."

"Is that true? Actually how many serial killers have you nicked?"

"Well none but if I did I am sure they would be eating carrots and wearing Hush Puppies. Look it stands to reason. If you are out and about doing a bit of random mass murder as a hobby you don't want to draw attention to yourself do you? Now brown shoes says, middle management and your wife buys your clothing. You probably wear a cardigan under your suit jacket because she worries you will catch a chest cold. The carrots say you care about the environment and your fellow man. Perfect cover for a serial killer, stands to reason."

"Are you serious?"

"It is a theory, granted a pretty rubbish one. What colour shoes was John Nightingale wearing?"

"Mandy thought for a moment. "I don't recall. Were they brown then?"

"I am only the DS here I assumed you were on top of this sort of vital information. What sort of detective are you anyway?"

She was forced to laugh as they turned into High View. John Nightingale was waiting for them in the garden. As they approached Mandy could not help but look at his shoes, brown. Sam saw her look at his feet and grunted. They remained two metres apart sat on garden chairs.

"There are a few minor points we should like to clear up," she began. "We have done a little digging and there are few facts that have come to light regarding your past. Do the names  John Night, John Knight, Nigel, I could go on, mean anything to you?"

There was a moment's uncomfortable silence while he considered his reply. He finally smiled. Mandy had to admit he had a sort of, humour and warmth to his manner which had no doubt served him well in his chosen occupation as a con man. "Yes I am sorry about that. I should have told you when we first met and saved you the effort. I assume you picked it up from the fingerprints you took from Sybil's room?"

Mandy ignored the question. "So tell me the details and save me the effort."

He smiled. "I am getting on a bit and I am finding difficult to obtain patronage. I thought where is there a plentiful supply of widows that might need a bit of companionship."

"And Eastbourne jumped into your mind." said Sam.

"Of course, easy access from London and knee deep in elderly women whose husbands have popped their clogs leaving them minted. So off I went. I rented a flat and set my stall out."

"So June Pulford was just a random choice?"

"It was clear she had a few bob. I can tell by the shoes and clothing. She wasn't buying stuff from the charity shop. That much was for sure. She liked to come into town and wander on the Pier. It was a bit tricky at first as her friend Sybil was usually with her."

"Why did you not target her? Why June Pulford, both as you put it were minted?" said Sam.

"I know you might find it hard to believe but not every woman is drawn to me."

"It's probably the brown shoes," said Mandy.

John look puzzled but continued. Anyway I saw that I had made a connection with June. We swapped email and phone numbers and then we started to chat. We arranged to met and so on."

"So how were you going to get your hands on her money?" Sam was to the point if nothing else.

"I am not admitting to anything criminal. There is nothing illegal in friends helping one another out. So in answer to that I had no intention to take part in any form of criminal deception."

"Look we all know that you are what's known to us coppers as a first class scumbag. However , that is far step from being a murderer. So let me explain how this works. I won't troll through every minute detail of you sordid life until I have enough evidence to bang you up for a nice long time and you in return will cooperate. So as one old pro to another I give you the one chance to do this the easy way or the next time we meet you will be off for a long holiday at Her Majesty's Pleasure," said Sam.

There was a moments silence while John Nightingale considered the alternative. "There is no need for unpleasantness. It is not that complicated and I assure you murder was nowhere part of the scheme. I was hoping if all went well to persuade June to perhaps move in with me. Perhaps move out of High View and live in a nice little villa in Spain or France."

"How might I ask would this be paid for?"

"Well fifty fifty of course, my share coming from the sale of my flat in Eastbourne when it competed."

"The sale of the flat that you don't own and that you are five months in arrears with the rent when June Pulford paid for you to move here?"

"You have been doing your homework," he said.

"So let me guess," said Sam. "There would be some sort of hold up with your sale and June would be persuaded that unless you acted promptly you would lose the chance to buy your villa on the continent. You persuade her to transfer her money into some sort of joint account to complete the purchase. There is some sort of g;itch. You have to fly off to wherever, to deal with it and lo and behold she never hears from you again and the money vanishes with you." said Mandy.

He remained silent. Sam spoke, " and Sybil, I am guessing she was onto you?"

"She didn't like me and suspected from the beginning that I was not all that June thought I was. So.."

"So you killed her," Sam finished the sentence.

"No I did not. I went on a charm offensive. I even bought her some of her favourite perfume and put it in her room."

"How did you buy it. We have checked you credit card there was no such purchase. You were isolated here so you certainly didn't pop to the chemist."

"Tom bought it for me."

"The gardener that has a side line in growing weed in the potting shed?"

"I don't know anything about that. He just helps the residents out that is all. I gave him the money and he went to Boots the chemist and bought it. Tina Thorndyke uses him to pick up the non prescription stuff like aspirin and ointments. He was going anyway so as well as getting my booze and fags I asked him to pick up a bottle of her perfume."

"Did it work? Was she changing her attitude to you?"

"Quite the opposite, I got Elvira to let me into her room to surprise her with it. She decided that I had been in their on the rob."

"How unjust, " said Mandy sarcastically.

"Too right," John Nightingale broke into a broad smile. "Anything else."

"You can go," said Mandy.

"I am guessing my romance is over with June then?"

"It will be in the next half hour or so," said Sam.

John shrugged and wandered off, "Oh well back to the drawing board," was his parting comment.

# Chapter 23

June Pulford was upset, very upset. Sam was looking bored. Mandy could see, that not the most patient at the best of times he had had enough of the grizzling and would soon say, get a grip or words to that effect. She did have some sympathy for June. Anyone would be upset to discover the  person they thought to be the love of their life was nothing more than a second rate con man, would be.

Mandy had deliberately decided to interview in this condition while she would be still emotionally distraught. At this point she judged that June, rejected and humiliated would be mostly likely to reveal anything she knew about her formal best friend.

Sam now having endured a couple minutes of self pity decided it was time to get on with it. June sat in the same chair, in the garden that John Nightingale had occupied ten minutes earlier.  "So it has come as a bit of a surprise that Mr Nightingale was out to con you?"

Mandy looked at him and the phrase bull, 'china shop' sprang into her head.  It did have the desired effect in that June look up and gave Sam her attention, albeit she did seem quite annoyed.

"Of course it did. I thought I had at last found someone after all these years. We had plans.."

"Well he certainly did, to relieve you of your money," interrupted Sam. Mandy rolled her eyes in disbelief at Sam's bluntness and June started crying again.

"I know it's a shock." Mandy gave Sam a stern look warning him to keep quiet.

He shrugged and his face adopted the an expression that said, "what, what have I done?"

June gathered herself and began to speak. "I still can't believe it. He said he was just a temporary hiccup, when he sold his flat he would be in funds and then we would get a place together. Was it all lies?"

"I am afraid so," said Mandy as gently as she could. "He has form I am afraid. This would not be the first time."

"I paid for him to come here. It seemed a good temporary solution. Of course with the pandemic we were more or less stuck then."

"It probably saved you, " said Sam. "I am guessing that by now he would have disappeared having managed to persuade you to put all your money under his control on the pretext of buying a villa somewhere in Spain or where ever. "

"Will you be charging him?"

"We will refer it to a specialist unit. We are looking into the murder of Mrs Meadows," said Mandy. "We would like you to fill in as much detail as you can for us. You can start by telling us about her and John. Did she suspect that he was conning you for example? What did she say?"

"Sybil didn't warm to him from the very start. She told me that there was just something about him. I said that he was just one of life's nice people. Her exact words were. " if it's too good to be true then it usually is." She annoyed me. To be honest I thought she might just be being selfish. You know she wasn't happy about me moving out of High View and leaving her."

"I suppose up until John's appearance on the scene you were close and he broke that up for her."

"That's true. I spent more time with him and I have to be honest I did neglect my friendship with Sybil. In a way it was selfish or at least thoughtless but I enjoyed meeting with him. It was a change, I just felt life had a bit more, what's the word, sparkle. He was a breath of fresh air."

"Can you tell me the precise details as to how you came to meet. You told us earlier that you bumped into him on the Pier. Do you think it was purely accidental, chance?"

"How could it not be?"

Sam took on himself to explain. "This is not the first time he had done this sort of thing. It takes a great deal of time and effort to win someone's trust and confidence. You can't just wander up to someone and ask for their money. It is from his point of view a long haul so he would want to know that his victim was worth the effort, worth the investment so to speak."

For a moment Mandy thought that June would start to cry again. Subtlety was definitely not Sam's forte. June carried on though. "I remember the day we met well. It was Tom's idea to go into Eastbourne that day. I didn't usually go on my own but Sybil's daughter was due a visit. He said he was going in and had an Uber booked."

"Tom Wellbeck, does he have a lot to do with the residents as a rule?"

"Not really, he Is usually in the garden doing bits and before lock down he would run the odd errand and that sort of thing. Anyway he seemed a nice enough chap and would always make a point of talking to Sybil and me. He was just very friendly."

"So how was it you actually met John that day. You said you spilt an ice cream on him?"

"The taxi dropped Tom and I on the front. He said he had a little time before his appointment and why not have a walk on the Pier. We decided to have an ice cream and started to queue at the kiosk at the entrance to the pier."

"So how come you were by yourself when you met John?"

She paused for a moment. "Oh I remember. That's right. We were in the queue and Tom pulled out his mobile phone. It must have been on silently and buzzed. It didn't ring. So he walked away from the queue to talk on it. Then he came back and said he had to go. He was in a rush and said he would met me at the entrance to the pier in hour and a half."

"And that's when you and John met? What a fortunate coincidence for Mr Nightingale that you just happened to be there," said Sam.

Mandy spoke. "You obviously had strong feelings for John. It is equally clear that your friend Sybil had completely the opposite reaction to the man. In fact I understand that things came to head in the residents lounge. In fact the tenon between you seems to have reached almost violent levels. Can you take me through the precise order of events that day?"

"We were in the lounge John and I. He had cut his hand, somehow, the day before. I know he had been talking to Tom in the garden and went to the where the sheds are. Perhaps he scratched it there."

"Did he say what he had been doing?"

"He had asked Tom to get some perfume for him to give to Sibyl. So he had this cut and I could see it was infected. I decided to get some antibiotic cream I had in my room. When I came back Sybil was telling Tina that John had tried to or had broken into her room. The door to Tina's office was open. Sybil came out and walked into the lounge just ahead of me. Dr Passmore and Elvira were tending to him,"

"And that's when the row between you and Sybil kicked off?"

"As we entered she said that she had proof that John was up to no good. I was furious and lost my temper. I said some regrettable things but at the time she just seemed to be poking her nose into my business. I am sorry now."

"You weren't so angry that you decided to poison her, by any chance?" said Sam.

"No of course not," she replied.

Mandy and Sam watched her head back inside. "What do you think?" said Sam.

"I think that we need to speak to your weed growing friend in the potting shed," said Mandy.

# Chapter 24

Sam and Mandy waited in the garden at High View while Tina Thorndyke went off in search of Tom Wellbeck. "There are some nice flowers here," said Sam.

"You are just making conversation now," said Mandy.

"I was thinking of retirement. I might start gardening as a hobby."

"Do you have an interest in it then? I didn't have you down as gardener?"

Sam muttered, "No not really, I don't really like the outdoors, too much chaos and disorder. I prefer a nice neat bit of concrete. It was just a thought. What about you?"

"I had a horse, well a pony when I was younger. I loved going out in the countryside for a ride."

"How posh can you get? Don't tell me you and your dad used to go out, ride across the estate and make sure the peasants were hard at work."

"I am not posh and we didn't have an estate. There are bridle paths all over the countryside. You don't have to be rich to have a pony."

I had a bike that I used to ride over the waste ground behind the block of flats where we lived. That is until somebody nicked it."

"And that's when you decided to become a copper to see the bad guys caught?"

"No not really, it was when I got caught nicking a replacement and got the living daylights knocked out of me by the kid's dad whose bike it was. He was the local copper. That's when I decided being a policeman was a good idea."

"So you thought the policeman had behaved badly in using violence against you and decided that you would do better and set a higher standard. That's a very good reason to join the force."

"Sort of , the copper had bashed me with impunity so I thought if I became a copper I would get hold of the kid who had nicked my bike, give him a good pasting and I wouldn't get nicked. I was only nine at the time."

It took Mandy a while to work out that Sam was winding her up. He was usually grumpy and it always took her by surprise when he made a joke. Before she had a chance to respond Tina Thorndyke appeared. "I can't seem to find Tom anywhere. I think he has left."

Sam and Mandy roused themselves and got to their feet. "Let's have a look in the shed in the rear garden," said Sam. The three of them walked to the back of the building and made their way through the foliage that hide the outhouses from view. Sam opened the door to the shed where Tom had been sleeping. The sleeping bag, clothes, belongings and his stash of weed had all gone.

"Yep," said Sam, "he has definitely done a runner."

"Can you get us his employment records," said Mandy.

Tina Thorndyke hesitated. "I don't really have any."

"And why would that be?" said Sam knowingly.

"He was just casual so I sort of paid him cash in hand."

"Of course you did and why not? Saves all that messy tax stuff, all that bother of checking passports and identity not to mention that tedious legislation dealing with, minimum wage and national insurance." He was annoyed.

Mandy was more pragmatic, "tell us what you know about him. "How did you come to employ him."

She thought for a moment trying to recall. "He just turned up on the door step."

"And you just said would you like a job as a gardener and by the way I am going to pay you less than the statutory minimum wage?"

"No of course not. He saw the grounds were in a mess. You see we used to have contractors that managed them. But .."

"But, let me guess you couldn't afford to pay them so they cleared off and you saw the chance of getting it done on the cheap."

"I suppose so. He offered to do some gardening and see how it went. He did a good job and so I kept him on."

"And you don't have any details on him at all?"

"Sorry, nothing," she looked nervous. "Will you be taking the matter further?"

"I honestly don't know. You are not helping matters very much are you. One thing is pretty clear though. Honesty is not one of your core values is it Ms Thorndyke? I am now certainly having real problems in believing your explanation as to why over four hundred thousand pounds went from Mrs Meadow's bank account to yours."

"I protest.."

"Go and do it somewhere else will you ?" said Sam, "And in the meantime go and round up Elvira. Bring her to the front lawn where we can have a chat with her."

She left and they made their way back to their makeshift interview garden table. "I am convinced Tom has a lot more to do with this now," said Mandy.

"It definitely looks that way. He certainly seemed to have set June up for the meeting with Nightingale. He suddenly decides that he will take her into Eastbourne, disappears on a so called appointment then Nightingale befriends her."

"I agree. It makes sense. He and Nightingale are in it together. Tom wheedles his way in here and gets as much informations as he can on the residents. They then select their mark, June Pulford in this case. He sets her up for Nightingale to move in on."

"Can't prove any of it. We have no idea who this Tom Wellbeck really is, so proving any sort of link to Nightingale won't be easy," said Sam.

"As we dig into Nightingale further their connection may well come to light. I still can't see Nightingale poisoning Sybil Meadows though even if she had turned up some evidence to demonstrate to June that he was conning her."

"It is a big leap from con man to murderer but who knows people change," said Sam.

# Chapter 25

Tina Thorndyke reappeared in the garden. "I can't find Elvira anywhere."

Mandy glanced at Sam before speaking. He was clearly as surprised as she was at the news. "Are you saying she has vanished?"

"Exactly that. I have checked around and no one has seen her since last night."

"We need to check her room. Sam and I will put on our PPE and you should clear the residents from the rest of the building into the lounge so we minimise any contact." Tina scurried off to make the arrangements. Sam and Mandy made their way to their car. The boot contained clean sterile sets of personal protective equipment for their use.

Gloved, masked and wearing eye protection they made their way into High View. Tina meet them and maintaining a two metre distance led them to Elvira Mercado's room. The staff were housed in the attic rooms. There was a shared bath and toilet squeezed in between the small rooms. "How many rooms are there?" said Sam.

"There are four rooms and six staff have sleep here since the outbreak started. They are the only ones that have direct contact with the residents. Cleaners, cooks and the like come in but do not make any contact with the residents, the six carers or myself. The only person that has contact is Dr Passmore to administer to their medical needs."

"Does Elvira share her room?"

"No she was one of three that remained here permanently prior to the Covid outbreak. They worked a shift system so there was always someone on call around the clock. Some had to double up but she didn't"

They entered her room. A quick glance around confirmed that draws and wardrobe was empty. "Well she seems to have done a bunk," said Sam.

"Did anyone see her leave?" asked Mandy.

"No she just seems to have upped and left in the night."

"Okay what is going to happen next is that forensics will be examining the room to see if there is any evidence of anything happening here. In the meantime I need the key to the room. This is now a potential crime scene." said Mandy.

"If anyone saw anything please ask them to contact us." said Sam.

Sam and Mandy left and made their way back to the station and waited for forensics to arrive and do their job.

"Can I have everyone's attention please," said Mandy loudly in the incident room. "Let's do a quick once over and update to see where we are at."

Sam took over. "History and what we know so far, then what we need to find out, so Victim first, Potts."

"Sybil Meadows, unremarkable but with a wealthy husband and sitting on a fortune. Two kids who benefit, her daughter Stephenie married to Jeffrey Foster and a missing step son from her husband's first marriage, Michael. The other people who benefited from her death are Elvira Mercado and Tina Thorndyke. Elvira get a small legacy in cash and Tina avoids having to justify the so called investment in her business."

He paused and referred to his notes before continuing." We have dug into Jeffrey's affairs and it is clear that he was desperate for money in his failing business. We know that Sybil had enough of it and was not going to bail her daughter and husband out any further. We know there was an argument when this was made clear to Stephenie."

"Merryweather interrupted, "and we know she had the opportunity leaving vitamin supplements for her mother to take. We saw how easy it is to get arsenic on the internet. She could easily have doctored the pills. She had the means, the motive and the opportunity."

Sam spoke, "we can't rule out John Nightingale and this Tom Wellbeck." He filled the team in on what they had learned.

"So with what  we have the following scenario could have played out," said Siskin. "Tom Wellbeck gets a job at High View and is the advanced party, so to speak. He targets June Pulford as their mark and engineers a meeting with John Nightingale. Their plans to relieve her of her cash are delayed due to lock down. This gives Sybil time to follow up on her suspicions and is about to expose Nightingale as a con merchant. He gets wind of it, goes to her room and leaves the poison."

"Tom Well beck, undoubtedly an alias as Tina made none of the usual employment checks, has now disappeared. We now only have Nightingale's version of events and no way of tracing this Wellbeck Character," said Mandy.

"Tina Thorndyke on the other hand is very much on the scene. We have dug into her affairs and there is no doubt that High View is bust. Without the cash injection from Sybil she was going down the pan. Conveniently for her we have no way of proving theft against her. Sybil's death was certainly convenient, as was the wrong cause of death issued by Dr Passmore," said Potts.

"There is no doubt that he was either extremely careless or he deliberately put the wrong cause of death on the certificate. There is no doubt that he and Tina are romantically involved. There is no way for us to prove that he did not make a genuine mistake though. It is not uncommon after all." said Mandy.

"Either way Tina had a good motive and getting drugs is pretty simple for a doctor," said Sam.

"Except both Tom and Elvira have done runners. Forensics have done a sweep and there is no evidence of foul play. So it seems that they have both just decide to make themselves scarce," said Merryweather.

"Well I don't have them down as a couple, so why have they both disappeared at the same time."

"I can tell you why She had done a bunk," said Potts. "Her fingerprints taken from Sybil's room have turned up a match."

"I thought only Nightingale threw up a hit," said Sam.

"Not the criminal database, immigration," said Potts. "She is an over stayer, her visa has expired. She us not allowed to work."

"Ah Tina Thorndyke's casual approach to employment law comes into play again."

"Yep, no tax, no national insurance, no pension, no sick pay and cheap labour, How could she resist?" said Potts.

"Well that explains why she wanted to avoid us, It was only a matter of time before we would find out and then immigration would be looking to deport her as soon as they could. In the meantime I am guessing that she would be held in a detention centre. Given the circumstances I would make myself scarce. Track her down we need to speak to her again," said Mandy.

"Michael Meadows," said Siskin. " I have a bit more on the guy who murdered is own wife for running off with him, Trevor Drew."

"Well fill us in," said Sam.

"It is quite a sad storey really. So as you know Patrick Meadows abandons his wife and small son Michael and runs off with Drew's missus, Elenor and between them it seems that they steal all of Trevor's share of the money. There is quite a lot of background stuff on their business. The bottom line is that they were smuggling and dealing in so called blood diamonds coming out of Sierra Leone. It is fair to say that the pair of them were pretty unsavoury characters. Anyway Patrick leaves his wife Shirley and his son Michael and sets up with Drew's wife Elenor."

"Remind me what happened to his first wife, Shirley, " said Merryweather.

"I know what you are thinking, no she died before Patrick Meadows married Sybil. Her marriage wasn't bigamous and the Will is valid. "

"Just a thought."

Siskin continued. "We have found out what happened to Trevor and his son David. Trevor was sentenced to life in South Africa but he maintained contact with his son. In the latter years he even had day release and apparently his son would collect him and they would spend days out together."

"What despite the fact that his father had been convicted of his Mother's murder."

""He denied he had done it throughout the trial. I assume that his son believed him. By all accounts they were close. Then tragedy struck and his son died of a drugs overdose. Trevor identified the body and he himself then died in prison thee months after burying his son"

There was silence for a few moments. Sam spoke, "so if you think things are bad things for you remember things are a lot worse for other people. This Trevor Drew, losses his wife, gets banged up for her murder, loses every last penny and when he is coming up for release his son dies and he never makes it out."

"Well we need to find Tom Wellbeck and Elvira Mercado as a matter of priority." said Sam.

# Chapter 26

It was a hot sticky evening in Johannesburg. The bar was not air conditioned and located in the seedier part of town. Its patrons like the establishment they drank in were among the seedier part of humanity. It was hard to hear over the music and the conversation. Not all the clientele were there to have a drink, many came and left without even visiting the bar.

Michael and David sat at a small booth in the shadows. They had a good view of the door and the people entering. The customers in turn had a good view of them. A man or woman would enter and seeing them would nod or raise a hand before heading to the toilet area. They would be followed and the drug deal completed. The bar owner knew and received a commission for his tolerance.

"Have you been in Jo berg long?"

"All my life on and off. I get around though. I don't stay in one place too long."

The two men had met a few weeks earlier. Michael was being released from prison for a drink related offence and David had been visiting his father. A lift had been offered and accepted. One thing led to another, one drink to another and one drug to another.

Michael was soon a regular customer and David was only to happy to add him to the list of clients. He was not an ideal customer as he had no money. Gradually David set him to work, shifting the riskier side of the business his way. He would make the deliveries.

David rarely had drugs on him and if he did it was a small amount which he could claim was for personal use if caught by the police. If the bar was raided he would be found to be clean the gear carefully concealed in the toilet area. Even if located in a search there was no way to prove the stash was his.

Michael was out on the street transporting the drugs. He though if caught would receive the full force of the law. David paid Michael in product. He would consume most of it and sell some on his own account to provide essentials.

"Odd our paths haven't crossed before though."

"My mother died a while back and I inherited the house," continued Michael. "I sold it and had some fun. Money's run out now though."

"Well at least you led the high life for a bit. I have spent most of my life being an afterthought. I was fostered, stuck in children's homes and generally ignored."

"Life's not fair," Michael took a drink from his beer.

"You can say that again," he raised his glass and chinked it against his companion's glass.

The night wore on. " I best be off to make my deliveries," said Michael getting from his seat.

"Come round at about two and I set you up with the next load." He watched as Michael left the bar and headed into the darkness.

It was nearer three in the morning before there was a knock on David's door. He looked through the spy hole in the heavy reinforced door. He could make out Michael standing in the hallway. He began to undo the four heavy duty locks to his apartment. The door and the locks were designed with two aims in mind. One to give him time to get his gun and prepare to defend himself against any junkie that was set on robbing him and two to dispose of the gun and his stash if the police came calling.

Michael finally entered and the door was made secure behind him. It was clear that he was struggling from withdrawal and needed a fix. David waited.

With shaky hands he began to pile money from his pockets onto the grubby table located in the middle of the sparsely furnished room. David took his time counting the money carefully while his companion became more and more agitated. "Hurry up I am getting really jangly."

"You get squat until I am sure it is all here." As his companion became more and more agitated he continued to check the take, Satisfied he gathered the money and left the room. "Stay there," he said.

His safe was hidden in the floor of the bedroom. Checking that the door was shut and he was clear of prying eyes he unlocked it. He put the money in the safe, removed some white powder, locked it and recovered it with the carpet. He opened the door to the living area where Michael was still waiting.

He sat at the table and put the substance on the table. "This is special," he announced.

It was two days before his body was discovered. A regular customer having called a few times to get his fix had realised that something was not as it should be. He and a few like minded friends had returned armed with a crowbar and other useful housebreaking tools. They struggled but eventually managed to break into the apartment. The noise they made gaining access was ignored by the other tenants. They shared a common interest in having the police no where near them.

The body was already beginning to decay. They ignore it and began their search. The safe was located. They were unable to open it but they were able to prize it free. They left with their haul leaving the door hanging from the hinges and the body where they had found it.

One of the thieves who still possessed a touch of human decency decided to call the ambulance service albeit a day and a half later. The body was found and taken to the morgue. The death was certified as a drug overdose.

The police went though the flat and found a driving license, some correspondence and identified David Drew. After a week they located his next of kin, Trevor his father. As it turned out was easy to contact, serving time as he was for the murder of his wife. The police picked him up and drove him to the mortuary.

Trevor Drew stood over the body as the sheet was pulled back to reveal the deceased's face. He gasped and he trembled slightly as he looked down.

"Well," said the policeman.

In a barely audible voice," yes that is my son, David Drew," he said. He too would be dead within a very short time, dyeing in prison of a cancer that was already was growing within him even as he stood over his son's body.

# Chapter 27

Mandy finished reading the police report into David Drew's death. "What do you think?" said Sam. She and Sam were in her office at the nick.

"It is certainly a sad tale. Trevor Drew wasn't dealt the best hand in life. His partner, Patrick Meadows runs of with his wife, who without a second thought dumps her child and husband. Between them they steal every last penny and leave him to manage on his own. He ends up doing twenty years for murdering his wife and David is pushed from pillar to post from one foster home to the next. Despite all this he manages to keep contact with his son through thick and thin. Then to add insult to injury his son overdoses a year or so before he is due for release from prison. He never gets out and dies of cancer in a prison hospital."

"The thing that struck me though was the fact the David and Michael were associates," said Sam.

"I don't think it was an accident. Trevor Drew was an old lag and well entrenched in the prison hierarchy. I am guessing very little went on inside without him knowing about it. He undoubtedly knew that Michael Meadows was banged up there and he would have known that he was Patrick's son. It is not beyond the realms of possibility that he also knew when he was due for release. To arrange for his son to be visiting that day was also simple."

"So you think their meeting was anything but accidental?"

"I don't like coincidence and that is far too big a one to swallow. No the meeting between David and Michael was contrived." She read a portion of the police report into David Drew's death. "The police were very thorough in their investigation, surprising for what to them was just another junkie overdose. It seems that one of the junior detectives,

Nico Haan, had the bit between his teeth and was convinced that David had been murdered."

"I see that. The evidence pointed to at least one other person being present when he dies."

"And Detective Haan was convinced that it was Michael Meadows. His DNA and finger prints were everywhere. His reasoning was that David was a dealer and an experienced drug user. He knew exactly what he was selling, how pure and how strong, and yet.."

"And yet he had massive quantity of heroin and fentanyl in his system, in fact enough to kill ten people. I see," said Sam.

"His reasoning was that it was no accident and that the only person there was Michael Meadows. He followed every lead he could and that's why the report virtually covers every facet of their interaction from when they first met through their criminal activity together up to the death."

"But it couldn't prove it. It seems he was eventually pulled from the case." said Sam.

"So here's what I think. Trevor finds out his hated ex-partner's son is in the jail. After all these years he sees a chance to get even. He can't take revenge on Patrick who his dead by now but he can get at his son. He gets together with David and between them they come up with the plan for the two to meet."

"So what do you think the idea was?"

"I would guess David would bring Michael into his drug dealing business. Having gained his trust he would set him up with the police. It would then be simple to have him caught with a massive quantity of drugs. The courts there have a record of sentencing the major drug dealers to life and unlike here in the UK life means life."

"They intended to have him serve the same sentence as Trevor Drew."

"It would be a kind of poetic justice I suppose especially if Trevor as he maintained at the trial was not actually guilty of killing his wife, but that doesn't really explain why Michael would kill David," said Sam.

"I think Michael somehow worked out what was happening. Let's assume when he first met David he didn't know who he was but something happened that gave him away. It could have been anything a slip of the tongue or even a letter of something from the prison. Anyway he figures it out. He can be pretty certain that whatever David's plans for him are they are not going to be in his best interest. We can never be sure what took place that night in David Drew's flat but we can be sure only one person walked out of there alive."

"Somehow or another he was murdered with a massive dose of his own drugs."

"We have no idea where Michael is now but we do know he is a potential killer and all that stood between him and a fortune was one old lady, Sybil Meadows his father's second wife."

"But he is what about thirty, thirty one years old now, five or ix years older than his half sister Stephenie. We don't have a suspect in that age range who had access to Sybil, or the premises."

"I think we do. Your missing gardener, Tom Wellbeck."

"You think he is Michael Meadows?"

"It makes sense," said Mandy. "Let's say he travels to England and tracks his father's widow down and finds that she is living in High View. He contrives to get himself as a gardener and is waiting for the opportunity to speed her exit to the afterlife."

"Then the pandemic starts, lock down and he finds he can't get anywhere near her," said Sam.

"Sort of but the time line doesn't fit. He never had access to resident's rooms in High View. Tina Thorndyke might be tight and uses every trick in the book to save a few pennies but she is not stupid. She might have hired Tom on the cheap with no background checks but she certainly made sure he had no access to the Home and the resident's money and valuables."

"And," said Sam. "Tom was the one who took June Pulford into Eastbourne to arrange the staged accidental meeting with June Pulford, before the lock down was in place. That implies John Nightingale and Tom Welbeck were working together."

" And what if June was not their first choice? What if John Nightingale and Tom Wellbeck had a different plan altogether?"

"Sybil Meadows, you mean."

"Exactly what if the plan was for John Nightingale to charm her and at the right time and place arrange her death in a manner that would arouse no suspicion. Michael appears and claims his inheritance and John gets his share."

"That would explain Sybil's suspicions and violent dislike of John Nightingale. She had already met him before June brought him to High View. Tom had already arranged some sort of accidental meeting between them. She wasn't having it so they set up June."

"So when June introduced her new paramour Sybil knew immediately that there was a some sort of scam. She made it her business to put a stop to it."

"We need to have another word with John Nightingale," said Sam.

"I don't think so. We can prove nothing and he is far too experienced to roll over and confess. All we have is a suspicion that Tom Wellbeck and Michael Meadows are one and the same. That he somehow got to know John Nightingale. That they got together and murdered Sybil. We can prove nothing. We can't link them. We can't link them to the poison. We can't even be certain that Tom is Michael Meadows and we certainly can't prove that he murdered David Drew."

"So where do we go from here?" said Sam.

"We prove it," said Mandy.

# Chapter 28

Mandy was already in her office when the rest of the team started turning up for the day shift. Sam caught her staring into the middle distance. He had seen that look before and was about to leave her office without disturbing her train of thoughts. She jolted and saw him. "Sam," she said as though he had somehow magically appeared from nowhere. "Sorry, I was miles away."

"How long have you been here?"

"I couldn't sleep. I came in about five. Something is worry me and I can't put my finger on it."

Sam pulled up a chair and low and behold a bacon sandwich appeared from nowhere in his hand. "I find a bacon sandwich always makes me think better, don't you?" He smiled.

"I wonder if I could get your pet sandwich maker Bert locked up for assaulting a police officer with and offensive bread roll," mused Mandy.

"So what have you been thinking?" Crumbs began to appear on her desk as usual.

"I am thinking we need to go through the items recovered from Sybil Meadows' room," she stood up and leaving Sam to gather up his sandwich and crumbs, made her way into the communal area. Sam was puzzled at first until he turned and saw through the glass panel that a parcel had just been delivered to Potts. He realised that forensics had finished with their examination of the stuff taken from High View..

By the time he caught up with Mandy, Potts was reading from the list that was in the package. "Let's look at that," said Mandy as Sam came into earshot. Mandy put on gloves both as a precaution against coronavirus and also not to taint the evidence..

"What is it?"

"What does it look like?" she said.

"A photograph album," he replied.

"She resisted the urge to congratulate him on his powers of observation and began to turn the pages. "It is Sybil's late husband's, photos of his first wife and the usual. Look wedding photographs. I think that is Trevor Drew as best man. It is hard to be sure, from photos in the file we got from South Africa , but I am pretty sure that is the same man that is in the mug shots when he was arrested."

Sam studied the album. "Yes that is definitely him. Here look, roles reversed. Partick Meadows at Trevor Drew's' wedding."

Mandy flipped forward through the album. "See if you recognise anyone," she instructed. She continued to turn the pages slowly.

"Stop," said Sam. That's him."

"Who?"

"Tom Wellbeck," he replied.

"Are you sure?" she said. "I only saw him from a distance. You were the one that spoke to him."

"I am certain, that is him."

"Then it would appear that our theory is right and our missing Mr Wellbeck and Michael Meadows are one and the same," said Mandy.

She turned her attention to Potts. "Was the photo tested for prints?"

He began reading the detailed forensics report. "Not that I can see."

"Bag it and send it back to the lab and get them to take finger prints from the shed where Tom was sleeping," she said.

"Siskin, have you checked if Michael Meadows is in our system?"

"I have run every name in the case. There are a surprising number of Michael Meadows that have been nicked. As we didn't know what he looked like there was no way of narrowing them down."

"Sam sit down with Siskin, Go through the files and see if you can spot Tom Wellbeck AKA Michael Meadows."

"Merryweather drop whatever you are doing and cross reference all the prisons John Nightingale spent time in against fellow inmates. We need to put him and Meadows together at some stage. "

She left the incident room and picked up the phone and dialled. There was a delay before she was connected. Mr Harwood at Trent Styles and Pilcher finally appeared on the line. "What can I do for you detective Pile," he said.

"Just a few details in you would be so good? Firstly have you managed to contact Michael Meadows?"

"Not yet, we have placed notices in the Gazette and contacted a specialist firm of beneficiary hunters. We have also written to his bank. Apparently he has closed the account and they are unable to supply an address."

"What about the care worker, Elvira Mercado?"

"She has not been in contact either. I am afraid."

"One final question are you having an official reading of the Will?"

"I admit that did present some problems but as you know the Covid restrictions have been eased and with proper distancing we plan to hold it a week tomorrow."

She hung up and before she had time to take stock Sam appeared at her office door. "Got him, both Michael Meadows and John Nightingale were in the same low security facility together. Michael was done for drug related offences and Nightingale for an internet scam. We had the information from the beginning we missed it because we were looking for Tom Welbeck not Meadows."

"Passport details?" asked Mandy.

"He has a British passport. Both Patrick and Shirley were British."

"When and where was it issued?"

"A few months after David Drew's death, internet application verified by the Counsellor Service in South Africa. First one he had applied for."

"That is interesting. So if we are right in our theory is correct. Michael realises who David Drew is and that he is out to get revenge for his father. The tables are turned and he murders Drew. Things are getting too hot where he is and he decided to come to the UK. Old habits die hard and he gets himself nicked. While inside he meets Nightingale. The only thing that stands in the way of a big payday is Sybil , his father's widow."

"So they set out to murder her?"

" I don't think that John Nightingale knew that was the plan. His MO is not murder but conning women. I think he may not have known everything. I think Michael planned to kill her. If we are right he murdered David so we know he had no problem with bumping people off. No I think he sold it to Nightingale as a con. In reality he was going to murder her and set Nightingale up as the murderer."

"Which is what we have at the moment all the evidence puts him in the frame."

"It was simple on the face of it from Michael's point of view. Get a job at High View, contrive a meeting between Nightingale and Sybil. Kill her and blame it on him. Nightingale knew nothing of Meadows connection to Sybil."

"Except, Sybil didn't bite. So Michael gets Nightingale to focus on June Pulford. As far as he is concerned it makes no difference. All he knew was that Meadows had identified a mark for him and set her up."

"And it still worked for Meadows as long as Nightingale comes out as the prime suspect he was in the clear."

"Well that seems to be that," said Sam.

"Except," said Mandy. Sam optimism faded. "Except it doesn't explain the initial phone call involving us and the fake Will."

# Chapter 29

"Well Mr Nightingale, you do realise that you have been arrested as a suspect in the murder of Sybil Meadows. Please confirm for the tape that you have waived your right to a solicitor?" said Mandy. Sam and she sat one side of the table and social distanced on the other sat John Nightingale. The interview was being captured on the station's CTV.

"I confirm at this stage I do not want a brief but I reserve the right to change my mind at any stage," he replied.

Sam started the questioning. "I should like to explore your relationship with the young gardener at High View, Tom Wellbeck. How do you know him?"

"He is the gardener, he buys me my fags and places the odd bet for me."

"We think there is a little more than that. Tell me when did you for meet. I should like to remind you that we have full access to your criminal record."

There was a short silence while Nightingale gave the matter some thought. "Yes of course you do. Okay, we met when we were both doing a short stretch at Her Majesty's Pleasure."

"So you knew he was Michael Meadows?"

He looked surprised, "I don't understand. Who is Michael Meadows? I mean, I assume he is some relation to Sybil but I don't know him."

Mandy spoke for the first time. "We believe that Tom Wellbeck is Sybil's step son Michael."

"No that can't be right. I met Tom inside."

"Surely you must have known his real name?" said Sam.

"I know him by the name he gave me. We were allowed in the garden to have a fag break and that's where we got talking. He said his name was Tom. What do you think I then did, checked the register of births, deaths and marriage or asked to see his passport. Don't be ridiculous. He introduced himself as Tom. So guess what? I called him Tom."

"Are you saying you had absolutely no idea that Tom was actually Michael and that he stood to inherit a fortune on Sybil's death?"

John Nightingale went silent while he sifted the information. He was not a stupid man. It did not take him long to process it and understand the full implication of what he had been told. "You think I met this Michael in prison and entered into a plot to kill Sybil Meadows so that he would inherit. And then what? Split the money."

"That is exactly what we think happened. He got a job at High View and reconnoitred ahead. We suspect the original idea was that you would use your usual tricks to befriend Sybil. Once you had gained her confidence she would die in some unfortunate accident or other. Tom AKA Michael would have a cast iron alibi and you would on the face of it have nothing to gain from her death. Quite the opposite in fact, you would have lost your chance to swindle her money from her. You would have every reason to keep her alive until you had fleeced her. Once she was out of the way all Michael had to do was claim the money and pay you off."

"No, no," Nightingale was beginning to lose his confidence. "That was not what was to happen at all."

"Okay," said Mandy, "tell us what did?"

"You are right about the first part. As I said I did meet Tom and he told me there was this place he knew where there where old biddies just ripe for the taking in Eastbourne. He had somehow got to know the boss there, Tina as I found out later. Anyway he had it sorted that he was getting some sort of job there when he got out." He paused.

"When I got out he met me and said he had sorted a flat out for me in Eastbourne. He then brought one of the women into the town so I could accidentally, on purpose bump into her."

"Sybil Meadows?"

"Exactly, but she was having none of it. So he staged a meeting with June Pulford, She turned out to be the ideal mark, lonely, gullible and really looking for someone. Her husband had died and she was not the sort of person who liked being on their own. It was easy to ingratiate myself to you."

"You do know that you are a disgusting human being, don't you?" said Sam.

"Perhaps but I am not a murderer."

"Please continue," interrupted Mandy.

"Where was I, or yes," giving Sam a filthy look he continued." It made no difference to me Sybil, June or uncle Tom Cobbly and all. She was just another mark. I gave her the usual flannel. You know temporarily, short of funds, waiting for a lot of money to come through, start a new life together, buy a property, you know?"

"And she believed you?"

"Fell for it hook, line and sinker. So she agrees to pay for me to stay at High View. Then of course things start to go off script. The lock down is introduced. Bang goes the plan. There is no way of setting up the fake purchase of a home in the sun and getting her to transfer money to me."

"I don't buy it. You and Michael's plan was to bump off Sybil and share the money. Once on the inside you could easily slip her some poison."

"Except I did not not poison Sybil and I did not know Tom's real identity."

"What were you doing in her room?"

"I have already told you. I was leaving her some perfume. She was making trouble with June, ruining my pitch so to speak. I hoped to convince her that I was just a genuine, regular Mr Nice looking for companionship."

"That I am guessing was a bit of an uphill battle given the fact that you had already hit on her and been sent packing."

"Well that was exactly why I was trying to sweeten her. Clearly the dumb bit was that Tom and I staged the meeting with June exactly the same way. As soon as June described how we had met, Sybil's suspicions where aroused."

Sam spoke," surely that would be a motive for you to get her out of the way. Either way her death is very convenient?"

"I told you I didn't murder her."

"The problem we have is that, you had the motive and the

opportunity."

Mandy studied Nightingale in silence for a few moments before speaking. "I don't think you did. However I am pretty close to convincing myself you did kill her. There is definitely something you are holding back though."

"I have told you everything."

"No I don't think you have but in the mean time I am going to charge you by you own confession with attempting to obtain money by fraud or deception. I am tempted to hold you until you come clean but given your age and the nature of the Covid virus I am going to bail you. Don't think of taking a trip anywhere, if I have to come and find you I guarantee you will be held on remand awaiting trial with your previous."

The interview was terminated and he was taken to the front desk where he was formally charged and released on Police bail. As he left the station Sam turned to Mandy. "Why didn't you charge him with murder?"

"Not enough evidence for one thing," she said. "And I don't think he did it for another."

# Chapter 30

The mini heatwave that had hit the South Coast was making it very uncomfortable in the police station. There was no air conditioning. Using it would greatly increase the risk of spreading the Covid virus so open windows and perspiration were the order of the day. On the plus side the social distances measures had been relaxed making the police's job a bit easier. The case of Sybil Meadows murder seemed to have stalled with no new significant leads turning up.

Mandy sat reading the files for the third time. Sam was of the opinion that they should issue an arrest warrant for Tom Wellbeck. She on the other hand had a nagging doubt. Her thoughts were interrupted as Sam wondered into her office.

"Well where are we going with this?"

"We are waiting," she said.

"I don't see what for?"

"I am missing something."

"What is there to miss. Michael Meadows posing as Tom Wellbeck murdered his father's second wife to get his hands on the loot. One way or another he got John Nightingale to aid and abet him."

Just as she was about to reply the phone rang. She could see from the caller ID that it was Superintendent Taylor. obviously out of self isolating, he was back at work with renewed vigour. "DI Piles," she answered.

"Taylor here, I want to discuss progress in the Meadow's case."

"Yes Sir how can I help?"

"You could help greatly by making an arrest and presenting a case for the Crown Prosecution Service."

"I am not ready yet."

There was a long silence. She was used to the technique. It was not dissimilar to that employed by second hand car dealers. State you price and say nothing more. The seller is then left to talk themselves into the deal. She remained silent. Eventually she won the psychological battle.

Taylor spoke. "I am not telling you how to proceed. It is your case but all the evidence is pointing one way."

"As I said. I am not ready."

There was the sound of an exaggerated exhalation of breath on the other end of the phone. "What does DS Shaw think?"

"You can ask him yourself." She handed the phone to Sam.

Sam meticulously took a pack of wipes from one pocket and just as meticulously located the mini aerosol sanitiser spray from another. He then took some latex gloves from the box on Mandy's desk.

"Where is he?" Taylor was becoming annoyed.

"He is preparing to take the phone. He should not be too long. He has nearly managed to get his gloves on and has the wipes and hand sanitiser ready for the hand over." She almost laughed at Sam's over elaborate preparations.

Finally Sam was ready. He took the phone and cleaned it thoroughly with the wipes. Holding at a respectful distance from his ear he spoke, "DS Shaw, speaking."

There was a pause while Taylor spoke. Then Sam answered. "I fully agree with DCI Piles, Sir." Another pause while Taylor spoke again. "Shall I hand the phone back. I will sanitise it."

"He seems to have hung up," said Sam putting the phone down.

"I wonder why?" said Mandy. "Do you really fully agree with me?"

"I don't agree with you at all but that's got sod all to do with him," he said.

"Thank you," she said.

"No problem, you're the governor and in this job you you watch each others backs."

Siskin appeared. "Morning folks, it's all happening today. We have the lab report back on Sybil's photo album and guess what?"

"I'd rather not and I am not a lover of cheerful dispositions. So a, stop being happy and b, just tell us." Sam muttered.

"Sorry sarge I forgot your inherent grumpiness. They have found Elvira Mercado."

"Where and how?" said Mandy.

"London and immigration. Seems she tried to get a job but this time the potential employer was law abiding, unlike Ms Thorndyke and did their checks. They notified Immigration, she flagged up as wanted in our murder enquiry so they are shipping her down here under escort."

"That is kind of them, they don't usually do deliveries," said Sam.

"They have a van that does a pick up daily of immigrants who have crossed over from France in small boats. It runs along the coast and collects them. They are dropping her off here on their rounds. She'll be here anytime now."

"When she arrives set her up in one of the interview rooms. Sam and I will be down to have a chat. Now where's the lab report."

He left the report and she began to read. "Well?" said Sam.

She pushed the report across the desk to him. He sat reading, "I don't see anything. I don't know why you are so pleased with yourself."

"The photos," don't you see."

"They found John Nightingale's prints on the album. So what we already knew he had been in Sybil's room? There is nothing new here, Nothing we did not already know that is."

"Oh but there is. Look where they found his prints. It tells us everything. It tells us what he was really doing in her room. It had nothing to do with perfume and I think I know what happened."

"Tell me."

"Let's talk to Elvira first then I think we shall know everything."

# Chapter 31

Mandy and Sam made their way up the steps to the offices of Trent Styles and Pilcher, solicitors. It was just past nine in the morning but it was already hot. Sam was still moaning about the weather when Harwood appeared in the reception area. Mandy was finishing sanitising her hands. It was clear that all the Government guidelines were being meticulously obeyed, not surprisingly given that they were lawyers.

The rules on distancing had been reduced to one metre and gatherings with certain restrictions were now permitted. "We have a large meeting room where they will all gather at ten for the reading of Sybil Meadows' Will and the formal dissolution of her husbands trust.. They will be sat one metre apart and the room is well ventilated," said Harwood.

Mandy handed over a parcel to Harwood. "Sybil's and her husband's papers as requested."

"Are there any photographs and in particular of Michael Meadows?"

"The albums are all there. There is a form for you to complete so we can maintain the chain of evidence should we, at a later stage need to enter them at trial," said Mandy.

They followed him through to the room where the Will was to be read and the into a smaller anti room. "You can wait here until they all arrive."

"That is perfect," said Mandy.

"There is a coffee machine and biscuits," he said as he left the room and closed the door.

Sam made straight for the biscuits and immediately succeeded in covering the carpet in crumbs. "You would be the Hansel and Greta of the murder world. You realise that you would be the easiest criminal on the planet to catch, don't you?"

"I don't think so. You would never catch me." he said.

"I would just follow the crumbs from the crime scene."

Sam muttered something before returning to the table to select another biscuit. They became aware of voices in the next room. The beneficiaries had begun arriving.

Tina Thorndyke, June Pulford and John Nightingale had travelled from High View in Tina's car. There were a couple of off-street parking spots at the front of Trent Styles and Pilcher usually kept free for the partners but today one was made available to her.

The drive had not been the most pleasant. The tension between June and Nightingale was palpable. He had been reluctant to attend but the solicitors had insisted that all them were required. They followed the receptionist to the conference room and took their seats. There was no conversation between.

The door opened again and Dr Passmore appeared. Tina was shocked at his arrival. What are you doing here?"

"I am not sure but they were insistent that my presence was essential. I didn't bother to get into the technicalities. Why are you here?"

"The loan to High View apparently requires some sort of formal sanction and waiver from the beneficiaries."

The door opened again and Stephenie and Jeffrey Foster entered the room. "I didn't expect anyone else to be here," he said.

Before anyone replied Harwood appeared in the doorway. "Just seeing who was here."

Jeffrey was clearly unhappy at the assembly. "What are these people doing here?"

"There is the formal reading of Sybil's will to be dealt with. She has made some bequests. When that is done we can move on to the terms of Partick Meadow's trust which is a somewhat more complicated affair."

Jeffrey reluctantly took he seat along side his wife. "Can we get started," he pushed.

"It is not ten yet and we are still waiting for some further interested parties."

"That's pointless. No one has heard of or seen Patrick's son, what's his name, Michael in years. Just get on with it."

"Nevertheless we need to follow protocol in these areas despite you obvious desire to get to the substance of the matter." Jeffrey's face reddened with anger as he realised that Harwood had in essence called him greedy and grasping.

Before he could respond Harwood spoke again cutting him short. "Well I must go and see if there are any other arrivals but rest assured I shall be back on the dot of ten." The door closed behind him before Jeffrey could speak further. The atmosphere remained tense in the room and silence prevailed.

None present could resist the urge to keep looking at their watches. Time passed very slowly. The hands however moved closer and closer to the allotted time. There was no sign of Harwood at one minute to ten. Anticipation was mounting as they waited to see what windfall was coming their way.

They started as the door opened, breaking the silence. They all looked at the new arrival. Standing in the doorway was an uniformed policeman. Fear passed across the faces of a number of them. Following the policeman was Elvira and Harwood.

Harwood directed her to a seat. The officer spoke." I shall wait out side the door. You accept her release from police bail into your custody?"

Harwood confirmed he did and the officer left closing the door behind him. All faces were turned to her and most expressed surprise at her presence. The silence remained unbroken however.

Harwood looked at his watch and took his seat. In front of him on the long table, around which they all had gathered was the Will and allied paperwork. He cleared his throat and was about to speak when the door opened.

"My name's Michael Meadows and I am pleased to met you all again," said Tom Wellbeck.

# Chapter 32

Harwood waited while Michael Meadows took his seat. He then rose from his position at the head of the boardroom table and made his way to the door leading to the anti room where Mandy and Sam were. He opened the door. "I believe all the guests have arrived."

They followed him back into the conference room. Meadows was the first to react. He jumped from his seat and made a dash for the door. He pulled it open and was halted in his tracks. His exit was blocked by the uniformed officers that had escorted Elvira in to the meeting.

"Please take your seat," said Mandy.

"You can't keep me here against my will," he said defiantly and made to confront the policeman blocking his way.

"No problem," said Sam." Michael Meadows, I am arresting you for the cultivation and supply of a class C drug, namely cannabis. You have the right to remain silent anything you do say.."

"Alright, alright I get the picture," he made his way back to his seat."I want a lawyer though, if I am under arrest."

"Michael Meadows I am formally de-arresting you," said Sam. "Now sit down and stop being a silly boy." Meadows merely glared at Sam in return.

"I demand to know what is going on," said Dr Passmore.

"So do I," Tina joined the chorus of objecting voices.

"We are investigating the murder of Sybil Meadows so I think we can all agree that we all want the killer caught, don't we?" asked Mandy.

There was no response unsurprisingly."Good now first things first, Mr Harwood I think you need to identify Mr Meadows?"

"Thank you DCI Pile, I do indeed."

He addressed Michael Meadows directly. "I understand that you have never had any direct contact with the remaining members of you father's family?"

"No I have never met Mrs Sybil Meadows or Mrs Stephenie Foster my half sister. My mother however over the years, prior to her death sent my father, Patrick photographs of me growing up. I don't think he had any interest in me per se but wanted to be sure that I still lived and that he had to continue supporting her."

"The police have made available to me you father's photograph album which his window retained. I have to say that it makes my life a lot easier as there are a number of pictures in it showing you.. Given the other supporting evidence you have also provided I am quite happy as executor to admit your claim on the estate of the late Patrick Meadows."

Harwood directed his focus to Stephenie. "Do you at this stage wish to challenge? You can at any stage issue such a challenge to the Will and ask the courts to adjudicate but are you happy to proceed at present?"

Stephenie looked at her husband Jeffrey. He decided to speak for her,"just get on with it."

"Mrs Foster?" said Harwood.

"As my husband says," she replied.

"Very well but before I continue I understand that there are a few areas the police wish to clarify before I can proceed to the formal part of this meeting."

He gathered his papers and began to walk to the door."Detective Pile, Sergeant Shaw I leave matters in your capable hands." Allowing no time for the group to react he swiftly disappeared from the scene.

"It is nice to have you all together in one place," said Mandy. "It will make matters so much easier, don't you all agree?"

"It was patently clear that they did not and would all rather have been somewhere else. However, having been ambushed and placed in the situation no one was willing to argue and push themselves up the list as a suspect. Mandy moved to the head of the table to the position previously occupied by the solicitor. She sat herself down and Sam interposed himself between the assembled and the exit door.

"June Pulford, Sybil's closest and most loyal friend," Mandy began. "That is until John Nightingale appeared on the scene. Then the friendship began to breakdown did it not?"

June spoke quietly. "She was my friend I did not want her death."

"And yet you became so incensed that you almost attacked her in front of all the residents at High View," she continued. "She could not leave your relationship with John alone. Did she tell you that she had been approached by him first and that you were his second choice. Did that anger you?"

"You are right in that she wouldn't leave it alone. She was jealous and kept picking at it. It was none of her business. I tried to ignore it but the more I didn't rise to the bait the more she goaded. She told me that he was only after my money. She said that what other reason could there be. She asked me if I had a mirror and did I ever use it. If I did then it was pretty obvious that a man like John wouldn't want anything to do with an ugly old maid like me."

"So you lost it and decided to have it out with her?"

"I just had enough. She seemed intent on ruining what we had, John and I. She even threatened to hire a private investigator to look into his past. It was the last straw. All I wanted was her to stop poking her nose into my life."

"So you saw has destroying your last chance of a little companionship and happiness. So you decided to get out your life permanently?"

"No of course not. I just wanted her to leave John and me alone. "I didn't kill her."

"We shall see," said Mandy.

# Chapter 33

"Among you in this room is a murderer. All of you had a motive but one of you had means as a matter of course. I refer to you Doctor Passmore," said Mandy.

"Me, what motive did I have. You can't possibly believe that shoddy forgery of a Will. That was clearly a put up to frame me." He displayed all the indignation of a man falsely accused.

"The Will now that is very interesting is it not? It strikes me its existence gives rise to a number of possibilities. It was undoubtedly produced to point us in your direction. Yet it was clearly blatantly amateurish it its drafting. So what was it purpose?"

She paused not expecting a response and she received none. She continued. "We were convinced having attended High View that Mrs Meadows had died of natural causes and that the phone call that alerted us in the first place was perhaps the result of the fevered imagination of one of the guests. The appearance of the Will changed that and made us look more deeply into the accusation."

"We now have to confront a number of possibilities. The person who made the phone call felt that the matter had not been taken seriously enough by the police. Convinced that a murder had been committed the caller then decided to fabricate a piece of evidence, the Will to focus our attention on the murderer."

"There is the alternative that you, Dr Passmore.."

"I am not listening to any more of this nonsense. I don't need to be here." He jumped from his seat and made for the exit. Sam interposed himself and Mandy nodded for him to proceed.

"I am arresting for the knowing and fraudulently issuing a death certificate and body tampering. You have the right to remain silent.."

Mandy held up her hand to indicate to Sam that he should pause the caution. "Or you could just sit back down rather than coming to the station where you will face the questions under far more uncomfortable conditions and with the press involved, up to you?"

He made his way back to his seat and glared at her. She ignored him. "Where was I, oh yes. Another scenario which to me seems the more likely, is that having been questioned by us you needed to somehow cast suspicion away from yourself. Now being an intelligent man you realised pointing the finger at a third party was unlikely to wash especially if you were our prime suspect. So you came up with the idea of creating a really badly forged Will. This would immediately create the impression that you were being framed."

She looked at Dr Passmore. He said nothing and glowered back at her. "Fair enough, " she continued."The last possibility is that the Will was produced by a third party, not the caller and not you Dr Passmore. Having seen the police attend he or she feared that they would be caught. Bear in mind they could not have known that we had concluded there was nothing to investigate at that stage. In an attempt to obscure matters, fearing that they would be discovered he or she then makes a Will pointing the finger at Dr Passmore. The Will is then brought to our attention and Dr Passmore hopefully, from their point of view, becomes the prime suspect."

"So the key question that needs to be answered is who forged the Will?"

"Initially we ruled Dr Passmore out of our investigation. You had no motive. There was of course always the outside possibility that you had suddenly become a serial killer, who had just decided to go round bumping off the elderly. We looked into your years as a doctor and soon ruled that out. We could not see why you would kill Sybil Meadows."

"It then became clear that you are romantically involved with Miss Thorndyke It also was blatantly obvious that she was in dire financial straights and High View was on the verge of collapse."

Tina Thorndyke started her protestations. Sam spoke, "look you can either sit there quietly and answer DCI Pile's question or I can nick you under the Fraud and Theft Act and pop you in a cell until we are ready to deal with you, up to you?" She took a deep breath and gave up the attempt to feign indignation.

"Okay, let's get on," said Mandy. "Having delved into the finances it soon became pretty obvious that you, Miss Thorndyke had your hand in Sybil's pocket so to speak. So the question is did you, Dr Passmore poison her or did you cover up the cause of death because Tina had?"

She did not wait for the mandatory denial and continued. "That brings us to the cause of death, arsenic poisoning. That is not an easy poison to obtain. However we discovered that with a bit of savvy it turns our that virtually anyone could get their hands on it."

"Now here's the thing. You Dr Passmore were already in possession of medication that had arsenic as its base. You denied that you had any uncounted for. I ask you once again if that is the case. Before you answer please consider that we have sent the toxicology samples to a laboratory associated with Oxford University. They are at present busy in trying to develop a vaccine for the coronavirus but they will eventually test the samples. I have been assured that they will be able to identify where and how it was manufactured. So bearing in mind that if it came from the batches you had it will be identified forensically. So do you wish to amened your earlier statement."

There was a silence while he considered his position. "I cannot categorically say that the source of the arsenic did not come from me. It was an unusual set of circumstances brought about by the pandemic. I normally just act for the wealthy elderly as the regular doctor at a number of residential homes and a list of private clients. Most of my work is little more than showing sympathy and listening to their latest round of aches and pains. It is not cutting edge medicine and to be honest I am not really that up to date with medical matters. I found myself drafted into administering chemotherapy on behalf of colleagues. It was the obvious option in avoiding exposure to Covid 19 for the patients as it avoided the need to attend hospital."

He took a breath. He debated if he should take the next step and make a possible career damaging admission. "I would say that perhaps my recording and handling of the drugs was not of the standard one would expect."

Mandy was losing patience. "You are missing some poison, aren't you?"

"I think so but I can't be sure."

"Right, so when Sybil Meadows presented with the symptoms you were in a terrible position. You either had to come clean and accept that you had poisoned her owing to your incompetence or accept that some one had just helped themselves to arsenic that you casually left lying about,unrecorded and unaccounted for in your bag. So to cover yourself you signed a fake death certificate."

He said nothing.

"So that leaves us with two question. Did you poison her or did someone else? Finding yourself compromised did you just go along with it after the event or were you an active participant?"

# Chapter 34

Dr Passmore broke the tension. "I did not murder Sybil Meadows. There are other people that had a far stronger motive. What about her son and daughter?"

"As doctor Passmore suggests, Mrs Foster did you kill your mother?" Mandy asked.

"Don't be ridiculous," Jeffrey answered for his wife.

"Perhaps you, Mr Foster tampered with the vitamin pills without your wife's knowledge?"

Jeffrey was again close to losing his temper. "You can't prove any of this."

"That is an interesting response," said Mandy. "I may or may not be able to prove anything but just on the off chance let's examine what I would need to prove, shall we?"

Sam had moved closer to where Jeffrey was sitting. Social distancing or not he made his present felt to pre-empt any more aggressive outbursts.

"It is fairly obvious that you like to be in charge, Mr Foster. You see yourself as the man don't you? Part of the macho military culture you picked up in the army along with some medical training was it?" She held up her hand to signal she did not require a response and to anger him further. She was goading him, hoping he would say something that would incriminate himself.

"It must have been very demeaning going cap in hand to a woman each time you made a mess of things, especially a silly old woman. You must have been so frustrated with her. She just could not see what a brilliant business you had. Could she?"

"A little more capital and it would be a really successful enterprise.."

"It always needed just a little more investment though didn't it. Sybil realised that you were a hopeless businessman. You would never make money. It was never your fault things didn't work out. It was always circumstances, bad luck or somebody else's fault, never yours. Isn't the truth that basically you were dependent on your wife and her mother's income. You couldn't run the proverbial booze up in a brewery. Could you?"

Jeffrey was seething with anger. His face was turning red and he was almost snarling at Mandy as she spoke. Without warning he sprang to his feet and erupted into uncontrollable rage. Sam had anticipated it. Before Jeffrey could clear his seat he had his arm locked behind his back and pushed him face down onto the board room table. "Now Sir I would suggest you calm down before things get out of hand."

The door opened and two uniformed entered having heard the commotion. The positioned themselves either side of him as Sam released his grip. "Are you going to be a good boy?" asked Sam.

"Stop it, stop," Stephenie was almost in tears."Can't you see? Can't you see? All of this is because you can't face facts. You are not a businessman. Just be you that's all I have ever wanted. Stop trying to prove something that doesn't need proving."

Jeffrey slumped back into his seat. Mandy spoke more quietly and less confrontationally. "So you find yourself with a collapsing business. The banks won't lend you any more money. You have remortgaged the house. You are about to lose everything including your pride. The only thing that stands in your way is a stupid old woman. After all she has never had to do anything in her life. It just feel into her lap didn't it?"

She paused waiting for a reaction. There was none from Jeffrey or Stephenie.

"All she did to get rich was to marry Patrick Meadows." There was still no reaction from Stephenie. It was not lost on Sam or Mandy that she had not sprung to her own mother's defence. "A man that had made his money by stealing his partners, Trevor Drew's money and abandoning his wife. While you had served your country and worked all you life for what? To end up having to beg for handouts."

"And you Stephenie, had a tremendous row with your mother. She made it absolutely clear that there was no more money. She told you in no uncertain terms that she was not going to fund your waste of space husband any more. Was that when you decided to get rid of her? Was that the final straw, standing on the drive at High View in front of everyone being humiliated? Was that the moment that pushed you over the edge and you handed the pills laced with arsenic to Tina Thorndyke ?"

"No, no that was not how it was. I was upset but I didn't murder her"

"But you did give her the tablets. So Mr Foster did you doctor the pills without your wife's knowledge? Is that what happened?"

"No, I admit I had enough of the stupid old woman. It wasn't even her money in the first place. She only had that control because of the way her husband had constructed his Will. She had no right."

"Sadly she had every right. She was just protecting her daughter from a husband that clearly had little sense or self control."

"Even if we had wanted her dead where would we get arsenic?"

"Not a very good defence," said Sam. "Do you not think that we would not delve into the details of your business?"

Mandy took up the questioning. "As DS Shaw said we know full well that you have access to wide range of chemicals in the normal course of the business. You could have acquired arsenic at anytime in the past. Anyway anyone could have obtained arsenic with a bit of effort from the internet. You have the medical knowledge from you stint in the military. So you knew what you were looking for"

"You had the motive, the opportunity and trust me if you had the means I shall prove it. If you or Stephenie have at any point obtained arsenic we will find when and how you acquired it. We shall check every order on the Internet, every penny spent on your cards and every last shipment of chemicals to your company."

# Chapter 35

The atmosphere in offices of Trent Styles and Pilcher was so thick it could almost be cut with a knife. Mandy knew that by exposing every detail of Sybil's murder and scrutinising those present pressure would be building in the guilty. She knew who the murderer was and all the evidence only pointing one way. She also knew that others were lying, These lies needed to be exposed for they covered the truth and risked the murderer walking free.

"Tina we know why you would have an interest in the convenient and timely death of Sybil, don't we?"

"That is outrageous and ridiculous. My dealings with Sybil were purely business and above board."

"And yet her lawyer, Mr Harwood only became aware of these so called business transactions when he examined them after her death. It strikes me, were I to enter into a deal costing me nearly half a million pounds the first thing I would do is talk to my lawyer and make sure the paper work was in order."

"I told you I was arranging for contracts to be drawn up. There was a delay due to the coronavirus outbreak. Perhaps you haven't noticed but most businesses have had to close."

"A lot of businesses have closed but many have been able to function quite successfully with staff working from home, including solicitors and accountants. Now here is the odd thing, Ms Thorndyke, the lawyers who act for High View have been able to offer almost a full service even at the peak of the lock down and yet they have no knowledge at all of any transaction between you and Mrs Meadows. In fact they say the last communication they had with you was regarding putting the Company into administration. How do you explain that?"

"I did have discussions along those lines but Sybil offered to help when she became aware of the problems so I didn't follow it up."

"Nor did you instruct them to draw up any agreement for you and her?"

"I was busy with dealing with virus and safeguarding the guests. I did not know she would die so in my mind there was no rush."

"But you had time to access her bank account and transfer funds to yourself."

"I admit it was not ideal but in my mind it was only a matter of dotting the i's and crossing the t's."

"Or it was just the matter of helping yourself to her money."

Tina became red in the face and feigned indigence."You can't prove that. It was a business deal."

"So you keep saying but I shall tell you what actually happened and how you actually run your business. When residents move in as part of the paperwork you arrange for direct debits to be signed on their bank accounts and even more you have them sign a continuous credit on their credit cards."

She interrupted, "that is standard practice. We need to ensure their fees are paid on time."

"I agree but here is the difference between High View and say how a telephone company might operate their direct debits or continuous credits. They don't just take what they want. I have had the credit card team look into the matter. They have contacted all the banks of the residents, all their credit card providers and obtained all your banking records."

Tina Thorndyke's confidence began to slip for the first time. "You can't do that."

"It is a murder enquiry and I assure you that all the appropriate warrants and court orders were legally obtained. So the situation is that for many years you have been using the resident's bank accounts and credit cards as your own. Holidays, nice clothes and even your car was paid for using their money."

"That's just silly. That would have been easily spotted. I would have been reported to the police ages ago."

"Do you think we haven't investigated this type of fraud before? How it operates is simplicity itself. If some one picks up on it you claim it is a mistake by the bank or the credit card company and say you will sort it out. You then take the money from one of the other victims and repay the first. They are probably even grateful for your help in sorting it out. You then suggest that perhaps to avoid people taking advantage perhaps it would be a good idea if you managed their account for them. That is exactly what happened in Sybil's case. You have almost total control over her finances. With internet banking once you knew her pass codes you can do what you like. You change the access codes so she could even sign into her account. You then download her statements amend them and print them. To all intents and purposes when she looks at the statements you printed, her money in still there."

"That's just nonsense."

Mandy picked a sheet of paper from Sybil's effects handed to Harwood earlier. "We found this in her room. She held up a bank statement. All forged and printed by you. You have been systematically been robbing the residents for years."

Tina said nothing. The colour had drained from her face. She knew there was no where to run or hide.

Mandy pushed on giving no time for her to answer. She turned her focus back to Dr Passmore. "Did you enjoy the four day trip to Las Vegas?"

"What?" he was taken unawares.

"The trip paid for by Tina. You were up to your neck in this as much as she was. Between you have been spending the resident's money for years. You claim to have a large private practice and specialise in elderly care. Now here's a surprise you would earn more driving a bus. We have been through you tax returns, showing you income and your bank accounts. There is no match. You are a wealthy man yet you earn nothing. When we compare the money stolen what do we find? Transfers that mirror the thefts. The pair of you have been robbing the residents for years."

He hung his head. "It just escalated. It wasn't deliberate. It was just a small amount at first. We were both struggling and we got talking.."

"Shut up you fool," Tina screamed at him. Sam put his hand on her shoulder making it clear that he was more than happy to arrest and remove her from the room. She realised that staying and hearing first hand what was said could only be to her benefit. She shut up.

Dr Passmore continued, "before I knew it I was in too deep. We had to keep going."

"So Sybil Meadows worked out what was going on? To keep her quiet you poisoned her and faked the cause of death/" asked Mandy.

"No I had nothing to do with her death. You have to believe me. I knew of course that arsenic could have been involved but I could not know for sure. I suspected that I had somehow muddled the chemotherapy drugs. I even feared that I may have accidentality poisoned her or that I had inadvertently given the wrong drugs to patients. Some one like Elvira might have poisoned her due to my mix up. In order to help out during the pandemic I was collecting all the various drugs from the pharmacy and taking them with me for all my patients. I just couldn't be sure."

"And you wanted to avoid an investigation because you and Tina had been spending their money. You thought you would just put down a repertory infection as the cause of death and nobody would be any the wiser. After all the whole system was stretched to the limit so the chances of it being picked up was remote to say the least," said Mandy.

# Chapter 36

"Now of course the biggest beneficiary's from Sybil's death are Stephenie and Michael but there is one other player on the stage and that is you Mr Nightingale. You, as we now now are a petty con man who freshly out of prison went straight back to your old ways. The stealing of large sums of money from lonely and vulnerable woman."

"A bit hash," said Nightingale.

"Never the less true," continued Mandy."This time you had a little helper in you scheme, Michael Meadows posing as Tom Wellbeck. You met in prison and concocted a scheme. One of you realised that some of the wealthier potential victims of scheme were to be found in high class residential establishments like High View."

She turned her attention to Michael Meadows. "You had made your way to the UK from South Africa with the specific aim of tracking down Sybil, you father's second wife. Things did not quite go according to plan. So what happened? How did you end up doing time with John?"

He thought for a moment deciding if he should fill in the gaps. "What the heck, it is not important so I'll tell you. You see it was getting a little hot for me there and so I decide that going back to England might be in my best interest."

Sam spoke. "You were mixed up in the death of David Drew, the son of your father's ex-partner Trevor. He was found dead from an overdose."

"He died of a drugs overdose, what can I say. Don't forget that I have had my struggles with addiction as well."

"Which is why you ended up in prison with Nightingale."

"As I said things did not work out as planned when I arrived here. I was very short of funds and selling a bit of weed seemed to be the only option."

"It wasn't just weed and it wasn't a little," Sam added sarcastically.

"These things do have a habit of escalating." he continued. "Anyway things were going okay at first. I rented a place and after a lot of digging I managed to track down Sybil."

"So what was the plan. You were just going to go and visit her in High View ans say what? Hi. My name is Michael. I'm your step son and by the way could you see yourself clear to advance me a few thousand pounds until you die and I inherit?"

"I must admit I hadn't thought that far ahead. Anyway I got myself nicked and banged up with John."

"Why weren't you using your own name?"

"Well I was obviously charged under my name but I had been using the alias of Tom when I supplied my customers. It is not a good idea to give out your personal details when your are dealing drugs. When I arrived at the prison one of the first people I bumped into was a customer also doing a stretch. He recognised me as Tom so I let it ride. I picked up the Wellbeck bit from the antiquated pipe work in the showers. There was an old stop cock manufactured by Wellbeck and company foundry works."

"I had no idea his real name was Michael Meadows, " interrupted John. "We got talking one day and he seemed really interested in my party trick of conning old ladies."

"Let me guess. He told you about High View and the wealthy widows who lived there." Said Sam.

"More or less as I have got older it harder to pick up a mark."

Michael carried on. "So between us we cobbled together enough money for a flat in Eastbourne. We didn't have a real plan. I just knew I had to blag my way in somehow."

"And Tina made it easy for you. Her proclivity to do things on the cheap and avoid tax or other legal niceties paved the way."

"There was a small ad on line saying a gardener was needed. I didn't directly apply for the job but turned up on the doorstep and said that it looked a bit of a mess and would tidy it up for a couple of quid."

"And she bit, offering you the job, cash in hand of course."

"Once I had my feet under the stable I set about befriending the old dears, running errands and that sort of thing. Anyway I even used to go shopping with them or go for tea. Finally I got Sybil set up to met John."

"But that didn't work out and you switched your attention to June Pulford."

John took up the narrative."She was lonely and took little convincing. She lent me the money to move into High View."

"You really are nasty piece of work, aren't you," shouted June.

He said nothing while Sam urged her to stay calm. "We can look what charges can be brought later but a murder in more pressing," he said.

"Of course by now the rent on the flat was well in arrears," said Michael.

"So you moved into the shed at High View and grew some marijuana to sell and keep you going," said Mandy.

He smiled. "It was purely for personal use."

"Of course, go on," said Mandy. "I still cannot see how this helped with getting money for yourself from Sybil?"

"Well it didn't. The plan was to set up a fake property deal and John and I would split the money we extracted from June. I had no part in Sybil's death."

"Do you know something," said Mandy, "I do not believe a word you have told me. You, Mr Meadows and you Mr Nightingale have overlooked a couple of key pieces of evidence. There is the Will trying to implicate Dr Passmore and Patrick Meadow's old photograph album."

# Chapter 37

Mandy picked up the album from the board room table. She flicked through the pages and selected  photo of Michael Meadows. "This is clearly you in your father's album. I presume your mother sent photos to him over the years to keep you in his mind and remind him of his responsibility as a father."

"I suppose she must have. I didn't know she had done that," said Michael.

"Now the odd thing about this one and the more recent photographs of you is that they have John Nightingale's finger prints on them. I had the whole album forensically examined. How do you account for that?"

John and Michael exchanged glances but both chose to say nothing.

"Okay let me answer that for you," said Mandy. "We need to go back in time a little though, to the day you were released from prison in South Africa and met with David Drew who had been visiting his father there.

"It was no coincidence that Drew had chosen that day to visit. He father Trevor knew you were being released. He was an old lag and knew everything that went down. He was serving a life sentence for the murder of his wife and David's mother, Elenor. A murder he says did not commit. He saw his chance to get even with Patrick Meadows, the man who had stolen his wife,  all his money and the man whose testimony had put him behind bars."

"I did not know all this when I met David," said Michael.

"Oh I think you did," said Mandy.

There was a silence in the room. Mandy picked up the story."David and Michael entered into a sort of partnership much like their fathers had, Trevor and Patrick and much like their fathers it was illegal. They smuggled conflict diamonds and you smuggled drugs."

"Then one night at David Drew's flat it went too far and a death occurred. The police finally arrived on the scene which had been heavily contaminated by a robbery and found the body. The body of a young man, in Drew's flat. They confirmed the identity of the deceased by dragging his already terminally ill father from prison. Trevor Drew then indented the body as his son."

"I don't see what this has to do with anything," said Michael.

"Patience," she said. "My problem is Nightingale's fingerprints on your photographs in the album in Sybil's room." she let the sentence hang in the silent room.

"I shall now tell you what actually happened in that squalid flat the night of the death. You deliberately mixed a lethal cocktail of drugs and gave them to that young man. It was no accidental overdose I believe it was murder."

"You can't prove that. I never killed David Drew."

"You are right I can't prove it and you did not kill David Drew."

"I don't understand ," said Sam.

"The person who died that night was Michael Meadows."

"That's rubbish," Michael began shouting.

"Shut up," said Sam, " before I shut you up."

Order slightly restored Mandy continued. "When Michael ended up in the same prison as Trevor Drew he saw his chance at revenge. He knew somehow that Patrick had remarried, moved to England and that Michael had all but lost contact. It was no great feat of detective work to find out that Patrick was dead and that he had left a Will that ultimately would make Michael a millionaire. Whether Michael knew or not there is no way of telling. In any event he seemed to have been unaware of his inheritance and carried on living hand to mouth, surviving on his criminal activity."

"So the stage is set. David Drew befriends Michael Meadows, gains his confidence and gives him a lethal dose of drugs. He makes himself scarce. His father identified Michael as his son David. David reinvents himself as Michael. It is all too easy. Michael has no passport. David applies for one using a copy birth certificate. His father dies and he takes a plane to England."

"You can't prove any of this," said David Drew. Sam placed his hand on his shoulder deterring him from becoming more active.

"I am sure when we compare your DNA to you father's held by the South African Police I shall have my proof," she said.

"Now Mr Nightingale what exactly were you doing in Sybil's room."

"I told you I was leaving her some perfume."

"I give you full credit for sticking to a story but I think now would be a good time to come up with the truth."

"You seem to know everything why don't you tell me," he said.

"I shall. David Drew's plan was always to murder Sybil and get his hand on what was rightfully his. The money that had been stolen from him and his father. He came to England with the sole purpose of killing her. One problem confronted him and that he knew from his talks with Michael that his mother, Shirley had sent Patrick photographs of the real Michael Meadows over the years."

"He couldn't gain access to Sybil's belongings. I am guessing he had reconnoitred before hand and was working on a plan when he was arrested and ended up inside. His meeting with John gave him the idea to make use of his particular skill of charming old ladies."

"As it turned out everything fell into place. He got a job at High View and John Nightingale moved in. All that was left to do was to remove the photographs of the real Michael Meadows from Sybil's album and substitute his."

"Okay you are right. I got Elvira to let me into Sybil's room on the pretext of leaving her perfume and swapped the photographs," said Nightingale.

"And left your fingerprints," said Mandy.

"I didn't know that he intended to kill her. He said that he was going to pose as her step son who she had never seen and see if he could get some money out of her. He said it was worth a try and if it didn't work it didn't matter. I thought it was just another con. I knew nothing about all this stuff in South Africa. I thought we were just trying to con as much money as possible."

"But then she is murdered and we became involved. And you my friend are left holding the baby." said Mandy. "There is only one thing left to be done and that brings me to the forged Will."

# Chapter 38

"I don't know what you are waiting for. It is obvious that Michael, David whatever is name is killed my mother," shouted Stephenie.

"Yes why haven't you arrested him?" added Tina.

"Let's have a little bit of decorum," said Sam using his best police "let's be having you." voice. Mandy stood waiting for the commotion to settle.

"Well you see there is a little more for me to consider. I would like to take you back to the beginning. The day the row erupted between June and Sybil, the day Dr Passmore was treating John Nightingale for a cut to his hand. DC Shaw would you be so kind as to refresh our memories from you notes.

Sam went through the motions of looking at his note pad. Mandy knew what he was going to say before he started. It was to be the sequence of events that day but a compressed version of all the participants individual statements.

"Dr Passmore was in Ms Thorndyke's office preparing to leave having done his rounds. They were interrupted by Elvira Mercado. She asked if Dr Passmore had time to have a look at a cut on Mr Nightingale's hand."

"Elvira Mercado returned to the resident's lounge where virtually all the residents, about eighteen in total were gathered waiting for lunch to be served," he double checked his script before continuing.

"John Nightingale was sat at the far side of the room by the French windows overlooking the garden. Elvira had left the office and joined him waiting for Dr Passmore to finish talking with Tina Thorndyke."

"He was treating him when Sybil Meadows entered the lounge. June saw her approaching and left Elvira, Dr Passmore and Nightingale to confront her. There was an argument and Elvira went over to the two women to diffuse the situation."

He paused and saw that Mandy was closely inspecting the assembled group. She was looking for a reaction. The killer would know that the noose was tightening. He began to read again.

"Dr Passmore not wishing to become embroiled in the argument was in the process of making a speedy exit when Tina Thorndyke appeared bringing his medical bag. A brief discussion took place between the doctor and Tina. Then he left."

"Thank you DS Shaw," said Mandy."And there we have the whole thing," she continued. There were blank stares around the table.

Sam spoke, "Tina Thorndyke, I am arresting you for the murder of Sybil Meadows. You have the right to remain silent any thing you do say may be later used in evidence.."

"This is nonsense it was clearly Michael Meadows and John Nightingale," she interrupted the caution.

"You may wish to revise that statement after I present the evidence. Would you care to sit and listen or we can finish this at the station?" Tina sat back down.

Mandy picked up the narrative."You will note from DS Shaw account that all of you except Michael then posing as Tom, Stephenie and Jeffrey were in the lounge. The only person not there when the row erupted between Sybil and June was Tina Thorndyke. She was left alone in the office with Dr Passmore's bag containing the lethal chemotherapy drugs."

"You can't prove that I took anything from the bag," shouted Tina.

Mandy waited briefly for silence to descend. She turned her attention to Elvira. "I think it's time we had a little chat. Why don't you take us through it."

Tina interrupted again."Why don't you charge her, she had motive and the opportunity."

"Well if you listen to what she has to say then it will be obvious why."

Addressing Elvira Mandy said, "did you know that Mrs Meadows had left you a small legacy in her Will?"

"No, she never said anything about it to me."

"Of course we only have you word for that. Mandy then spoke to the suspects around the table. "i think we should just listen to Elvira's account of what she did and I think you will see why I ruled her out."

Mandy spoke to her. "Please tell me about you and Mrs Nightingale."

"Elvira started to speak. "When Mr Nightingale moved in he was like a breath of fresh air he was so happy and charming. The only person who did not like him was Sybil. He said that he needed to do something to make her happy."

"And you told him about her running out of her favourite perfume?"

"Yes, I suggested that getting her some might make her more happy with him. He spoke to Tom and somehow he came back with some."

"And you used your pass key to let him into her room?"

"I did but as soon as he was in he closed the door on me, leaving me out side. He took a very long time, far too long to just to put a bottle of perfume on her table. This worried me."

"You of course, you had no way of knowing that he was actually going through the photograph album replacing pictures of the real Michael Meadows with those of David Drew so naturally you became suspicious of him."

"That's right. Then Sybil died and I heard Dr Passmore talking to Tina. I only caught a snatch of the conversation but he was saying something about he should really involve the police."

"Of course he was in a dilemma he could not be sure that he had not poisoned her himself, he had been totally negligent in keeping track of the drugs in his possession. So he turned to his lover. Tina and confessed his concerns. She urged him to keep the matter covered up," Mandy interrupted before telling her to continue.

"So now I am thinking that Sybil may have been murdered and the doctor and Tina are going to keep it quiet to keep their and High View's reputation clean"

"So you decided to call the police and who did you think might have poisoned Sybil?"

"John Nightingale he was in her room for so long and he had a bottle of what he said was perfume. On hindsight I thought that he must have put it in her drink or something."

"Then you saw DS Shaw and me speaking to Dr Passmore and it was clear that we were not going to follow it up further. What happened next?"

"Mr Nightingale came and found me. He asked what I had done. I told him that I had head Tina and the doctor saying Sybil was poisoned and that I knew that he had put poison in her room. I don't know how it came about but he said that he would prove it wasn't anything to do with him. He said we should search Tina's office for proof that she and the doctor had done it."

"So you waited until Tina was otherwise engaged and you made your search?"

"Yes,"

"And what did you find?"

"We found a Will showing that Sybil had left everything to Dr Passmore. I took a photograph on my camera."

Mr Nightingale now would be a good time to account for this so called Will," said Mandy.

He coughed clearing his throat before speaking. "I suppose you are right there is little point now in hiding the truth. When you turned up at the care home my first though was that I had been rumbled that you were about to cuff me for trying to con June Pulford. I didn't know that Sybil's death was suspicious. It was only when I spoke to Elvira that I found out Sybil may have been poisoned and that she called the police. I had no way of knowing that when you drove away that the matter was closed. I thought forensics or someone would be coming and that I would be in the frame. Elvira made it perfectly clear that she thought that I had killed Sybil because she was getting in the way between me and June."

"So you typed up and printed the Will on your PC in your room?"

"That's right. I then persuaded Elvira to search Tina Thorndyke's office."

"Where low and behold you find the Will," said Mandy.

"Yes I just pulled it out of my pocket and dropped it on Tina's desk. I called Elvira's attention to it. She took a picture. Then as we left I just pocketed it and later threw it in the trash. Convinced that I was innocent and that the doctor had murdered Sybil, Elvira asked me to print a copy off her phone, which I did."

"And you sent that copy didn't you?" said Mandy to Elvira. "If you hadn't we would not be here now."

"Yes I sent you the Will."

"Then you realised that you were a key witness and would be investigated fully. That is when you had to disappear because you had overstayed your visa."

Tina became agitated, "You don't have any proof. This proves nothing."

"Prior to coming here I had the chance to take a full statement from Elvira. Would you tell everyone what you told me?"

"It was the day Dr Passmore came and as you say. The argument broke out between Sybil and June. I went over to where they were fighting. Where I was standing I had a clear view into Tina's office. The door was open. What happened did not register at the time. I saw Tina looking through the medical bag. She was reading the labels on various bottles and then she put one in her pocket before closing the bag and taking it to the doctor."

There was silence for a moment. "You can't prove that it was arsenic I took from his bag it could be anything," said Tina.

"Just a moment, don't go anywhere.

She walked to the door of the anteroom where she and Sam had waited earlier. She went inside and returned with two clear plastic evidence bags. "We tracked the rubbish collection from High View to the tip. The forensic team have spent a messy few days but eventually found what they were looking for. I told them to look for discarded Trisenox wrapping and container and the Will printed by John Nightingale."

"And guess what?" said Sam.

Tina was beaten."My fingerprints on the Trisenox."

"And only John Nightingales prints on the fake Will."

She looked like a woman defeated. Her body sagged into the chair and she hung her head. "It was spur of the moment. Earlier I had heard a snippet of conversation between Sybil and Stephenie. She was saying something about employing a private investigator. I knew now that she was talking about Nightingale and she suspected that he was conning her friend June."

"You thought that she had cottoned on to you plundering her bank account?."

"Yes, I saw the bag. Everyone was looking at June and Sybil having a go at each other so took opportunity to take the poison. It was easy to slip it into her food."

"Then you persuaded Dr Passmore that he had been careless with his prescribing and that he had given you the wrong drug. He was caught between the devil and the deep blue sea. If he owned up to negligence then his and you stealing would come to light and you would both be facing murder charges."

Sam opened the door and the two uniformed officers entered and took her into custody along with Nightingale, Drew and Dr Passmore.

# Chapter 38

Mandy left the interview where she and Sam had obtained a full taped confession from Tina Thorndyke. She and Sam had no sooner entered her office when the phone rang.

Sam looked at the caller I.D. "How does he do that?" Does he have some super power that tells him where all his officers are at any given moment in time."

"Taylor?" said Mandy.

"Who else?" He handed the phone to Mandy.

"DC Pile," she said.

Taylor spoke. "That was a job well done, I have to say. Have you extracted her confession?"

"Yes Sir and her solicitor was present. All done by the book."

"I have to say I did think you were wasting you time at first but you were proved right in the end. Of course you were very lucky to recover the evidence from the rubbish tip."

"Sometimes things do go your way, I was just lucky."

"Good police work is not luck, so well done again."

"The press are waiting for a statement.. Shall I call a conference?" said Mandy.

There was a moments silence before Taylor replied. "I think you have enough on your plate. You will be glad to get a break. I won't put that burden on you. Just leave it to me I'll take care of the press for you."

"Thank you, Sir so thoughtful of you," she replied.

"I'll get onto it right away and again good work officer." The phone went silent. Mandy handed the receiver back to Sam.

"Let me guess," he said. "he wants to handle the press?"

"Of course," said Mandy.

"Well there are two thing to say for Superintendent Taylor."

"Go on."

"He hates spending resources but he loves to take credit for the results."

Sam paused for a moment . "Talking of resources .."

"What about them?" Mandy interrupted.

"I didn't know anything about a search of the rubbish tip or that the poison container and the Will were found?"

Mandy looked a little sheepish. "Remind me to lose those two evidence bags later before we hand the case over to the Crown Prosecution Service. There will be no need for them anyway. They have a full confession under caution with witnesses so she will plead guilty to get a shorter sentence."

"You are very sneaky," said Sam.

"Is that better than posh?"

# Other Books by Nicholas E Watkins

# The Eastbourne Murders

## Murder Most Christian

## Murder Lost in Time

# Tim Burr Thrillers

## Tanker
## Bank
## Dealer
## Oligarch
## Steel
## Hack
## Jade

# TANKER

Murder in Care

## Chapter 1

The Hilux pulled up outside the laboratory and parked. The Moon sat low on the horizon and the first red glow of dawn lit up the dry desert sky. All was still, save for the barking of a dog. Security for this sector of the storage facility was in the hands of the Iraqis. Despite being the only thing moving at that time of the morning, the vehicle had not been challenged and no alarms were sounded as it drove into the inner compound.

On paper, the security around the complex of buildings forming the oil storage facility near Basra was impressive. ISIS had looked at it on many occasions as a potential target, but determined that the security presence was too high and their losses would be unacceptable. The laboratory, situated in its own area away from the main buildings, was, in contrast, perceived as far less of a target by the owners. They had neglected it in their assessment of threat levels, so security here was far less comprehensive.

The occupants of the truck sat waiting tensely in the darkness. They were armed with assault rifles, they would have no hesitation in using them if the need arose. They were committed to the aims of ISIS and would happily die as Martyrs in achieving them.

One of the truck's occupants was no more than a boy of sixteen, but he had the hatred of a thousand years in his heart. His Father and Uncles had all opposed the British occupation. It was part of his being, ingrained from childhood. He had seen how the invaders had gradually been defeated, driven back into their compound and finally isolated into a small, defensive position at the airport. He had helped fire the mortars into their base. He had seen their defeat and knew they were weak. He believed, in the end, ISIS would prevail and the Caliphate would be restored.

His companion was slighter in build but older, in his mid-thirties and with a pock marked face. He had been part of Saddam Hussein's army when the invasion had taken place. When the Coalition forces had overthrown the Dictator, they had disbanded the army. It had left him with a gun and no income. He had no love for Hussein and the then ruling Ba'th party but, he at least had an income and had been able to feed his family. It had not taken long for him to become disillusioned with the so called liberators of his Country and he now saw them as an occupying force.

"He should be here by now," said the older of the two. He looked at his watch. They had been there for nearly an hour. They waited another twenty minutes before the door to the laboratory opened and light spilled out across the compound. They jumped from the cab and, slinging their rifles over their shoulders, ran to the beckoning figure.

"Quiet, follow me," said the man in the lab coat. The technician moved swiftly down the corridors, turning left and right. He used his security pass to open doors and led them further into the building. He stopped and pointed to the radioactive symbol and the warning sign above the door. "My pass will take us no further," he said, leaving them outside the door and returning to his job in another part of the building.

The young boy sneaked a look through the glass panel at the top of the door. "Be careful and keep your head down. What did you see?" said his companion.

"Five of them, they are putting their coats on and getting ready to go home." They knew their shift was due to finish at six a.m. the intruders' information was proving to be correct. Unsupervised, they had developed the habit of knocking off early. They waited quietly until the door opened and the workers began to gather up their belongings. The first worker stepped through the door, bidding goodbye to his colleagues. The boy leapt to his feet and struck him in the face with the butt of his rifle, smashing teeth and breaking bone. The technician staggered backwards into his departing colleagues, his hands clutching his bleeding face. The older of the two pointed his rifle at the group, moving it from side to side. They stepped back, dropping their coats and bags to the floor.

"Put your fucking hands down. This isn't a cowboy movie," he said. "You know what we want, so let's not make this difficult for any of us, OK?"

The workers looked at each other, their team leader, an American, decided to speak, "How do you intend to transport it?"

"Just stick it in a box or bag."

"You will be exposed to a massive dose of radiation. More than an hour or two and you will get very ill and possibly die. Do you realise that? This material needs to be handled with extreme caution."

"Do we look like the kind of people who give a fuck? Now stop pissing about and bag it up for us, unless you'd like to die before it kills us." The head technician began the process of removing the radioactive rods from the calibrating machines and placing them in boxes. He and another technician then unlocked the radiation proof safe and removed the rest of the material, stored for intended future use and put it in the bag along with the rods.

"Give us your cell phones." The workers did as they were told, while the duo ripped the internal phones from the walls. "Now, we are trying to let you live, but we need to escape without you causing us a problem. We'll lock you in and smash the key pad on the other side. We know that will only keep you in here for a very short while, but think on this. If you raise the alarm, all of you will be dead by this time tomorrow and all your families will be dead by the time you get home. You are all Iraqis, apart from this man and you live here. We know you. We know your families. We know where you live and we will kill anyone who betrays us." He drew a small pistol and shot the American head of department in the face to underline the message. The rest of the group cowered and watched in shock as their boss fell to the floor. They had the message loud and clear.

The two men walked out to the truck, struggling under the weight of their radioactive load. "Why are you letting them live? They could raise the alarm?" said the boy.

"The tall ugly one is my cousin."

********

At the petrol station at Qa'im, just inside Iraq on the Syrian border, two ISIS fighters waited in a Ford Galaxy mini bus that was rapidly becoming hot and sticky inside. They had been there for some time, one of them got out and relieved himself. He returned to the bus, "Do you think they are coming? They are very late."

"We wait."

"We are very exposed here. The Security Forces could easily pick us up."

"We wait," said the other with finality.

So they waited and finally the convoy of heavy trucks came through the checkpoint at the border. They were escorted by guards travelling in lightly armoured vehicles. Scant attention was paid to the convoy and they were, more or less, just waved past by the Iraqis. The border was like a sieve and smugglers for the Government and the opposing factions travelled virtually unhindered between Iraq, Turkey and Syria. Trade between the three was probably more vigorous than before the conflict had started. The region had descended into total chaos. Fighters were going one way and insurgents the other, guns in, guns out, drugs and Jihadi brides were passing for good measure. The whole area was a complete security shambles.

The convoy pulled over to swap the escort for the next leg of the journey. The drivers got out of the assorted trucks and HGV's, relieved themselves, ate, faced towards Mecca and prayed. The occupants of the Galaxy joined them in prayers. By now a small fleet of trucks and cars had arrived in the area. It was apparent, that on crossing the border, the truck drivers all had small business ventures going with various locals smuggling items from one side of the border to the other. The gas station had descended into a mini bazaar.

It was a very simple matter for the mini bus occupants to help the driver of the truck carry the large box and place it in the rear of the Galaxy. "Sorry for the delay lads," said the driver "got held up on the road. It seems there was a change in the group that controlled a stretch of the highway. It took an age to sort out the bribe to allow us to pass. It cost me another eight hundred dollars to deliver your goods."

They knew that he was bumping the price up and they guessed he had probably paid a tenth of that. They were in no mood to haggle and gave him the extra. The driver was almost embarrassed by their lack of bargaining, but he, of course, accepted the extra cash.

The Ford Galaxy pulled away from the stop and headed south. If anyone had pointed a Geiger counter at it, they would have seen the needle go off the scale.

******

There were three bombings in Baghdad that day and over a hundred people were either dead or injured. The hospitals were struggling to cope with the injured and dying. ISIS was under pressure and they had been losing ground recently. They were stepping up their bombing campaign, part in retaliation, but also in order to let the World know they were still a force to be reckoned with.

The University was in a state of chaos. A targeted bomb had left the Campus in disarray. Students and staff were among the dead, dying and injured. Ambulances, security forces, police and militia were all engaged in the action. Chaos and panic had spread across the Campus.

The three ISIS members were looking for the Metallurgy Faculty and referring to a map of the building. Soon, they located the secure facility. Security today, however, was totally lacking following the carnage outside. The combination of suicide bombings and the random shooting into the crowd of students had made anyone, with the slightest instinct of self–preservation, get well clear of the Campus. They marched along the corridor to the store of radioactive material and literally, just blew the doors off with a small, plastic explosive charge. They walked back out with a holdall stuffed with the deadly radioactive material, got in a car and drove off. ISIS had just gone nuclear.

Chapter 2

The rain dripped through the hole in the sun awning into the bucket placed on the terrace by the bar owner. There was a large puddle where the bucket had over spilled. A young couple made a dash for the café, the male, wearing flips flops, slipped and nearly fell. The female was more sure footed and reached their table in a less dramatic fashion.

The tables and chairs on the terrace outside the Terminus Café, were a random collection of plastic, cane and metal. They had obviously been collected and replaced over the years and were a total mismatch. The Patron came out and, nearly slipping and falling himself, emptied the bucket that was filling at such a rapid rate in the downpour, served little purpose. Tim looked at the sagging awning, the red stripes faded into the greying white background and wondered, given that the rip in the awning was no bigger than six or seven centimetres, why the owner had not applied a piece of duct tape. Perhaps duct tape was rare in France, or perhaps the owners just could not be bothered and accepted the heyday of the Terminus Café, located directly opposite Menton railway station, had long since passed.

Tim sat with his back to the Café with the open glass door to his right giving him a clear view of the terrace, the station car park and the coming and goings of those entering and leaving the railway station entrance. He stirred his double espresso, three sugars, too many. He kept meaning to cut down, but somehow, forgot each time he put spoon to cup.

To his left there sat the cowboys. Two almost identically dressed men with white beards, stained orange with nicotine. They wore black leather sleeveless jerkins, white stained T shirts and black faded leather cowboy hats with large cross stitching on the brims and crowns. Their sleeping bags and Worldly possessions were stacked under cover in a shop doorway to the left of the Café. Their hands shook as they lifted their coffee to their lips, which the patron's wife had placed on the table in front of them a moment before. They were obviously regulars. The dog that emerged from the Café ran to greet them and was instantly scooped up onto one of their laps by trembling hands.

On Tim's right was a large red and white bag on a chair. Beside it, on the table, were three further, smaller plastic carrier bags stuffed with old clothes. The owner appeared from the Café and stood by the bags. She was in her fifties, hair long and dirty. Her hands also trembled as she struggled to raise a cup to her lips. The drug and alcohol abuse were etched in her face and thin body. She was dressed in flimsy, floral patterned beach trousers, a leopard blouse and a beige wrap around cardigan. Her feet were dirty, her toenails uncut and her toes forced over and under each other by the large bunions on the side of her, flip flop clad, feet. At some stage she must have had a life and obviously had loved her high heeled shoes. Tim imagined her as a young girl, dressed smartly, with her designer shoes and handbags, going to the Casino in Menton, or dancing in the night clubs. No longer desirable, broken and addicted, all her possessions in bags, she relied on the Terminus Café for her morning ablutions. She hopped nervously around the table, taking alternate sips of coffee and dragging on a roughly rolled cigarette that occasionally stuck to her lips.

Tim took another sip of his very sweet coffee and looked up to see a group of four men running from a black van to the cover of the terrace. There was more slipping and sliding on the treacherous wet tiles before they reached the safety of the chairs and sat at a table. The bucket was now overflowing, as the rain continued to pour down. Thunder could be heard in the distance. The patron appeared with croissants and coffees and greeted the arrivals. Their jackets showed them to be railway workers. A fifth man dashed in and joined them and was greeted loudly by his co-workers.

So far, not one of the Café's customers fitted the bill of the man he was expecting to meet. He ordered another espresso and again put too much sugar in it. Tim, whose real name was Anthony Burr, had acquired the nick-name from his schoolmates. They had been unable to resist the opportunity for the joke, a "chip off the old block, timber," so the name stuck with him. He had been waiting at the Café for nearly an hour so far. Tim was forty one and looked out of place as he sat in the rain in the faded establishment. His clothes were a cut far above those of the other customers and his well-groomed appearance made him conspicuously noticeable. He felt uncomfortable.

This weekend had certainly not turned out as expected. He had anticipated spending a jolly few days at the Hotel Lewes in Monaco, watching the Grand Prix and perhaps getting a bit of sun. Today was race day and he had his place reserved on a nice yacht facing the track. Instead, he was sat, in probably the grubbiest café in the Cote D'Azure, doing someone else's job in the rain.

He had joined the civil service after he left Selwyn, Cambridge. He had done well enough, with a two one degree, to get a job in the Home Office. After a few years he was transferred to help out the long suffering Ambassador in Paris, where he would use his knowledge of foreign affairs to brief him daily with what was happening in the World. Technically, he was employed as an intelligence officer. Sounded like a spy but, in reality, he read the local papers, checked the briefings from the various government departments and made sure the Ambassador had a clear picture of the current situation and a clear understanding of what the current policy thinking was. After working in Thames House for a couple of years, he finally got Paris and was on this beano in Monaco. Along with the Ambassador, staff, some trade delegation chaps, he had managed to wangle the invite for himself to watch the Grand Prix, from a yacht booked by the Turkish trade delegation, in the Marina.

A note had been passed to the Ambassador's aide and as they had no one spare, here he was sat in the rain, waiting to meet a contact who, presumably, had a bit of inside information on trade or some such thing, while everyone else was tucking into a champagne breakfast on a luxury yacht.

He looked at his watch. His contact was late. The couple had left and the railway workers were making their way across the car park to the station. The itinerant cowboys appeared to be texting. How odd the World was. Nowhere to sleep, but you had a mobile phone. The table on the other side of the door was now occupied by a black man with a large suitcase on wheels, not his contact, a traveller perhaps? Not so, he clearly was the supply centre for the horde of beach hawkers that sold cheap goods on the beaches. He was approached by further Africans and goods were swapped around and money changed hands. The bag lady was looking at a mobile phone on offer from a beach trader, but there was still no sign of his contact.

The rain had stopped, the hills beyond were still bathed in a grey mist and rain and the distant sound of thunder could still be heard. He looked at his phone, checking the Grand Prix update. It was raining in Mote Carlo as well and the start of the race was under threat. He had now waited for nearly an hour and half. Enough he thought and made his way inside to settle up.

No one was to be seen, clearly service was not a priority at the Terminus Café. He heard voices from a side room. He stood and waited for a while. In the end, with no sign of anyone, he made his way towards the sound. He stood in the doorway. The family were sat around a table, covered with a red and white plastic check table cloth, having their breakfast. He stood. They looked quizzically at him. "The bill," he said.

Reluctantly, the wife got to her feet and making him feel as though he was a nuisance by being a paying customer, she walked to the bar.. He followed her. His French was poor, GCSE standard. He could not understand the number being requested and pointed to the till which should have displayed the amount or printed off a bill but did neither. This caused a blast of French. The till was clearly not in the regular habit of being used. Cash in hand was the order of the day here. He removed ten euros and offered it to her. Success, change and he tipped her fifty cents. He had to admit, that although not salubrious, the Terminus Café was value for money.

He turned to leave, feeling that the morning had been a waste of time and effort. "Monsieur pour vous?" she handed him an envelope from behind the bar. It was addressed "L'homme Angletere," vague but effective.

Outside, he pulled out the note and read." Hotel Belgique, Room 15, Rue de la Gare. After 10, the concierge goes at 9. Code 8476, Stereogram." His heart sank. He would have to come back tonight. This was not the fun break he had hoped for.

He realised he was already in the Rue de la Gare. He glanced down the road and could clearly see the Hotel Belgique. He considered the note. "Who calls them self Stereogram?" he said to himself as he made his way across the car park to the railway station.

The rain had stopped in Menton, at least. He had purchased a return ticket in Monaco, so he went straight to the platform. The train was on time, but crowded with race goers. The journey took ten minutes with two stops. Then the problems began. He knew he needed to buy his ticket now for his trip back to Menton that evening. The queues would be huge after the race. Leaving the train, he tried to make his way to the main ticket concourse, but was blocked by a group of race officials. The crowds were being controlled by the seat numbers to their positions around the circuit. He tried to explain that he wished only to purchase a ticket, but that was clearly not in the remit of the marshals who ushered him off in the opposite direction. The station, he had to admit, was spectacular, clad in pink marble and spotlessly clean. Despite its architecture and splendour, he was losing interest in its elegance as he walked the whole underground route to end up at the other end of the town.

The streets were packed with race goers, street traders and race officials marshalling the pedestrians. Everywhere was jammed and everyone, it appeared, was going in the opposite direction to him. The rain had started again and was tipping down. He was very wet and fed up by the time he finally made it back to the station ticket office. He finally bought his return ticket to Menton. It was nearly two o'clock by the time he returned to the hotel to find everyone had left for the yacht. A pass to allow him access to the Marina had been left behind the desk, but he would have to get himself there. The Ambassador and the rest of the party had a nice escorted limo drive. He, on the other hand, would be back in the crowd, marshalled and wet. He set off with his recent purchase of a grey and white souvenir Monaco umbrella.

## Chapter 3

Berat woke to the smell of tea, simit bread and the sound of hammering downstairs. His Mother was busy in the room next door, where she and his Father slept and where they all ate and watched television. Although it was just seven in the morning, he knew his Father had been up for hours working in the shop downstairs.

The whole flat smelt of leather, always of leather. They lived above his Father's cobblers shop. By the time he and his brothers were fed in the morning and went down the stairs to go to school, his Father would be busy at work. Piles of shoes were stacked up in the house, in the shop or outside waiting in pairs on the pavement, either for sale or collection. His Father was not the only cobbler in the street. The whole street up and down had the scene repeated. His trip anywhere, always started by passing between piles of footwear on the pavement surrounding his home in either direction.

His friends Emir and Ahmet were waiting to walk to school with him, He made his way past shoes and said goodbye to his Father who sat on the floor with a bradawl in his hand and a shoe on the last. His Father always said, "Work hard and get an education. You don't want to end up doing this all your life."

He took on board what his Father had said. So he had worked hard and had an education. Now a grown man, he sat on the wall overlooking the Bosphorus. The noise of the traffic on the road behind him was deafening. Vehicles of all shapes, sizes and ages streamed past, many blasting thick plumes of oil burning smoke. He suspected that Turkish emissions laws for vehicles, like many other laws, were not strictly enforced. In some ways the Country had come a long way since he was a child, in others it was going backwards. Ataturk, the Father of the modern Country, had created a secular government distinct from the religion. For a while, with the exception of the odd military coup, it had functioned, but now the State was more repressive and fundamentalism was on the rise.

Stretching in front of him was the sea, glistening with patches of oil and pollution. The oil tankers lined up to enter the Bosphorus, the twenty mile long north-south strait that joins the Sea of Marmara to the Black Sea and separates Europe and Asia. The ships were so large and appeared so close that you felt you could reach out and touch them. They seemed like toy boats in a bath. He had grown up with this sight all his life, but it still continued to captivate him. Now, in his mid-thirties, working as a civil servant, he longed for the simplicity in his life as it had been as a child, playing in the streets of Istanbul.

The Bosporus was just a part of his everyday life, from childhood he had taken it for granted. He remembered, as he gazed on the comings and goings of the vast ships, the day he had gone to University. His Father had gathered the whole family, brothers, cousins, aunts, uncles and friends to celebrate. His Father's pride was so great that he felt the burden to succeed weighing on him. He set himself to nothing but study and achievement. He did succeed, a first class degree followed by a masters and a well-paid secure job in government. He had taken extra language courses and spoke perfect French and English. He now travelled frequently around the World, acting as translator for the great and good in government and commerce. He knew that the English name Bosphorus came from the Greek bous, meaning cow and poros, meaning crossing, cow crossing. The legend went that Zeus had an affair with Io. When his wife Hera got wind of it she turned Io in a cow and created a horsefly to sting her bottom. It hurt so much that Io, the now cow, jumped across the strait.

He smiled to himself as he thought of cows jumping over the queue of tankers waiting to move oil around the Globe. His smile faded as he thought of Emir and Ahmet, brothers. He had grown up with them, shared school, fights, and sexual adventures. They were more like his own brothers or his family than friends. Their lives, of course, had diverged, he to University while they had remained in the grubby backstreets of Istanbul scraping a living as best they could. They were still close, but their life experiences were separated by a gulf wider than the Bosporus. He knew that, with their increasing frustrations and poverty, they had become more and more fundamentalist in their beliefs.

Behind him he could hear the call to prayers ringing out across the city. It was not that he was a bad Muslim, it was that he was more tolerant and inclined to live and let live. He valued peace. He had seen enough suffering acting as a translator around the Globe to know that the World did not need a helping hand down the road to more pain. Ahmet, the younger of the two brothers, had first become involved actively with the Fundamentalist Brotherhood when he was in his late teens. Like all young men, he had imagined himself the hero, fighting for truth and Allah, saving the poor, fighting the good fight. Berat reflected, as a child watching the old kids' television programs of jousting knights rescuing damsels, he had also seen its appeal. He knew all young boys yearned to be heroes and brave and the Muslim Brotherhood movement offered the chance to fight the corrupt and gain glory.

Ahmet started attending the more hard-core seminars held at the Mosques, meeting with other frustrated young men and searching the internet for like-minded individuals. It was not long before his brother Emir was being drawn into the more radical form of Islam as well. Now in their thirties, they wanted change. The idea of secular government was an insult to them, their beliefs and above all, to Allah. A trip to Syria had hardened their resolve and they were committed to the cause. Berat, to an extent, humoured them, not wishing to lose touch with that part of his life and his roots in the streets of Istanbul. He had been guilty, to an extent, of letting them think he was right there with them.

Celik, his wife was their younger sister. Berat had known her as the little pest that the three of them had teased as children. That had changed one summer when he came back from University. They fell in love and married. She was a good wife but shared many of her brothers' beliefs. Berat knew that, as her husband, she respected his wishes and never voiced her opinions to his more secular colleagues they mixed with.

As he sat watching the sun coming down and turning the sky bright red, yellow and lavender, it seemed to him that it was like an omen. His World was changing, he had not asked for it but it was. He now had choices, choices that Allah should ask no man to make.

Berat had been excited at being part of the delegation going to Monte Carlo. Of course, French was his specialist language and he would head the team of four translators working with him. It was a chance to influence the British. They all knew their support was key to Turkey's entry into the European Union. He knew that every opportunity would be taken to polish their record on human rights, their commitment to fighting terrorism and to demonstrate their commitment to the West.

He was finalising the details with his team when Yosuf had asked him to step into his office. Berat immediately sensed that this was not the usual, checking on final details, type of meeting.

"Take a seat," Yosuf commanded. This was unusual, Yosuf was not a command type of person. Berat feared he had made an error and was to be hauled over the coals. "There is a problem, a big problem," Berat feared that his job was on the line as Yosuf continued.

"You are married to Celik and she has two brothers, does she not, Emir and Ahmet?" he did not pause for a reply." "As I said, there is a problem." He seemed to struggle to find the words to continue. The word problem hung in the air. He took a deep breath. "They are to be arrested."

Berat's mouth hung open in surprise, "Arrested, for what."

"Security matters"

"My wife?"

"She will be fine, do not worry on that account; I have vouched for you both. I told them I know you to be a loyal servant of the State and totally dependable."

At that moment Berat realised his suspicions of Yosuf were well founded. He had always suspected that there was far more to Yosuf's role than just head of the Foreign Office translation department. He now realised, in that role, Yosuf could travel around and liaise with his Country's espionage resources globally. He had worked with him for nearly seven years and this confirmed that he was definitely part of Counter Intelligence. With hindsight, Berat began to see historic events in a new light, burglaries, disappearances and killings fell into focus. He was not just a translator. He was part of the cover for the State to carry out what it needed to do.

"You realise you must not warn them, nor tell your wife, don't you?"

Berat nodded, but he knew that he would and that decision would change his life for ever.

Yosuf knew he should not have warned Berat, but he was fundamentally a decent man. Turkey was such a contradiction. The State was becoming more oppressive, reversing women's rights and curtailing the media, on the other hand it was fighting a campaign against ISIS and terrorism. He knew Berat was a good man and he genuinely hoped that with this warning, he would keep himself and his wife well clear of her radical brothers. His hopes were to be in vain.

Berat knew he would betray his boss, even as he was warned to stay silent, but he also knew he could not stand by and not warn his wife. He left the office and changing trams had made his way to the Grand Bazaar. He knew this could be a trap to test his loyalty and feared that he may be followed. He hoped that the most crowded area in Istanbul would give him a chance of not being observed by anyone sent to follow him. He mingled in the crowds, stopped, doubled back and hoped he had avoided a tail if there had been one. He entered the phone shop.

Berat had purchased the cell phone for cash with credit on it. Sent the text to Celik warning her, with instructions for her to destroy her phone and dispose of the SIM card. All the authorities could trace then would be an anonymous text from an unregistered phone, but the content of the message could not be retrieved. Berat removed the SIM from his new phone, pulled out the battery and dumped it.

Celik ran down the road looking from side to side. She knew people were watching her. She was sweating and panicking. She ran as fast as she could. The text had been clear "Your brothers are to be arrested for terrorism. Do not use any phones, they are tapped, warn them and destroy evidence."

Her lungs hurt as she ran up the winding staircase to the flat where her brothers were. She banged on the door. The door opened onto a normal scene. "Grand Theft Auto" was paused on the PlayStation, they had been drinking coke and eating crisps as they played.

"What's all this noise," asked Ahmet, standing in the doorway dressed in shorts. "Is there a fire?" She pushed past into the room.

"The police are coming and you must get rid of any incriminating evidence, do not use the phones." The look of panic was in their eyes. Frantic activity began as she left.

"Take this. Someone will contact you for it," Emir pushed a

memory stick into her hand. She kissed her brothers and ran again. She was a street away when she heard the sirens.

When Berat arrived home he found Celik upset and distraught. She had followed his instruction to the letter. "They were arrested. I warned them and they gave me this." she gave him the memory stick. Berat plugged it into his computer, but could make no sense of its contents. He did know, however, what was on it should be in the hands of the State, but handing it over would put the final nail in the coffin of his own wife and her family. He could destroy it and not warn anyone, but he was sure that that would result in the deaths of innocents in their hundreds or more. The alternative of giving it to ISIS, when they contacted Celik, which they surely would, was also not an option.

## Chapter 4

The race was due to start at four and it rained like it can only rain on the Mediterranean Coast. Warm and wet, it continued to rain and then, as if on cue, the rain eased and the race started under the safety car. It did not take long before the drivers became bored with driving in convoy so they decided that the conditions were good enough and the air was filled with the full glorious roar of Mercedes, McLaren, Renault and Ferrari. It was loud, Formula 1 loud. The cars were a blur as they passed in front of the yacht. The Lady Heloise, moored in Monaco, was a hundred million dollars' worth of some one's toy that looked like it had never set to sea in its life.

She was moored at a beautiful location on the straight with bends visible at both ends. The Marshals in their red overalls lined the track along the quayside in front of them. The lower deck had been laid out as a dance and buffet area, while the upper decks were for the Brits and drinkers whose glasses were constantly filled with champagne. The lower deck was crowded with beautiful people. A video operator filmed the guests from every angle with a camera suspended from a gimbal and a stills photographer snapped incessantly. A black girl, with almost an afro, in a very flimsy bright yellow dress and her white friend in a bikini made sure they danced their way into every shot. Other young girls were scattered around like cushions to add to the décor.

Tim positioned himself on the top deck and watched the cars going round the track behind the safety car, He then watched as Verstappen crashed and his Red Bull car was hoisted clear off the track by a crane, as the race continued under the virtual safety car. The virtual safety car required the cars not to overtake and follow the car in front at a non-race pace until the green flag sign was illuminated, signalling full racing was to recommence. As the race resumed, Tim was approached by the Ambassador.

"Ah you made it? Sorry we couldn't hang on for you, but as you know there is the schedule to keep to in all these affairs." He smiled broadly as he spoke. He had a full face, a face that seemed to ooze affability and understanding and eyes that focussed on whomever he was speaking to, letting you know that you had his full, undivided attention. It made no difference if you were the cleaner or the Premier of China, that face was always totally absorbed and interested in what you had to say. He did actually sound genuinely sorry for leaving Tim to wander through the crowds in the pouring rain while he was chauffeured in luxury.

"No problem. I enjoyed the walk and needed the exercise," Tim lied.

Jason Delonge was your typical old Etonian, totally confident, comfortable in every situation and knew anybody who was worth knowing, added to that, he had obtained the trendy must have Philosophy, Politics and Economics first from Oxford, suits from Dege and Skinner in Saville Row and was set for all steam ahead in the diplomatic World of today.

Tim knew that Jason was actually brilliant at his job, but couldn't help feeling a bit irritated by how easy it had come to him. Tim also had his suits made by Nick at Dege and Skinner, but he always felt like he did not quite belong there and somehow the suits seemed to look better on the Ambassador. In truth the Ambassador had run to a paunch while Tim worked out in the gym daily and had practised martial arts since joining the society at Cambridge.

The conversation could only take part in short bursts in the brief relative quiet when the cars were not flying past. "How did your trip to Menton go?

"Nobody turned up," he picked the wrong moment to reply. Clearly the Ambassador had not heard a word, but by force of habit, seemed fully engaged.

"That's good then. You can sort it out on Monday with the naughty boys." He wandered off heading towards the decorations dancing on the lower deck. Tim turned his attention back to the Grand Prix. The naughty boys referenced were the attachés assigned by MI6. The spies every embassy had.

"Hi." He turned to see an oriental girl in her mid-twenties with a massive straw hat garnished with flowers, wearing what appeared to be a recreation of a Mary Quant lace mini dress. His eyes were automatically drawn to her chest where her nipples were clearly visible through the gaps in the crocheted work. She was stunning, too young, too obviously on the make but very pleasing to look at.

"Hello, are you enjoying the race?" he asked.

The roar of the engines did not make conversation easy. He did establish that she was planning to be an actress, model or something in PR and that she knew a great deal about shoes and fashion. Clearly they had a great deal in common. He liked the look of her body and she liked his career prospects and the fact he was divorced with no children.

He had met his wife at University and they moved in together for the second year in a house share. The third year at Selwyn meant he had a room in the College, so there had been a brief separation before they reunited in and moved to London. In hindsight, he probably would have done worse on his course if he had lived with her in the third year. She obtained her first without breaking sweat. She had the brains. They married when they got to thirty and planned on children.

Then it all started to go wrong. Lisa's career went cosmic. A whole new world, she was a banker, then a fund manager. He saw the change in her. There was nothing he could do. He knew he was boring, pedestrian, and irrelevant. She was dynamic, energised and a winner. They were no longer the people they were at Cambridge. They were now poles apart. The divorce had been quick, more painless for him than for her. But life goes on.

He looked at the girl standing beside him and decided that life was not going to go on with her that day. He made his excuses and watched as Roseberg lost pole allowing Hamilton to go on to win.

In the office on the lower deck, the translators, provided by the Turks, were lacking in co-ordination and leadership. Yosuf was furious. "Where the fuck is Berat?" He shouted at his aide.

## Chapter 5

Booking the Hotel Belgique had taken Berat a few clicks the night before and there had been no queue at Mote Carlo for his return ticket to Menton. It was early Sunday morning and most of his colleagues would just be making their way down for breakfast. He made his way along the long marbled halls to platform two. The platform was virtually empty. He immediately spotted the Englishman from the British group waiting for the same train. He recognised him from the cocktail party on the Friday night and the qualifying session which they all watched from the Lady Heloise. They had not spoken, but he was pretty certain he would recognise him in turn.

He had not expected this turn of events. He, in no way wanted to be identified as the source of the information. Turkey was a member of NATO and shared intelligence with the other member States. One slip and his name would be out and the Turkish authorities would know that he had aided his brothers in-law.

He sat down on the benches that were positioned at intervals along the platform. Unlike most seating on station platforms, they did not face the rail track but were positioned at right angles facing the bench opposite. There was a middle aged man and a teenage girl sitting opposite him. They were very engrossed in each other. Berat now had his back to Tim.

Berat's mind raced. He needed to rid himself of the memory stick, memory sticks to be accurate. He had taken the precaution of copying the original. He could feel them like two enormous weights in his jacket pocket. In hindsight, his plan of meeting a British agent in a hotel room seemed a bit simplistic. Pass an anonymous note, meet a spy, dump the information and go home to a normal life. Now it seemed far more complicated. True, he wanted to prevent the deaths of innocent people at the hands of ISIS, but he did not want the source of the information traced back to him and his wife,

He jumped as a train rushed through the station without stopping, shaking him from his thoughts. His stomach churned with nerves and he felt himself sweating, despite the cool of the subterranean platform. He took several deep breaths in an attempt to calm himself. He needed to come up with an alternative plan that did not reveal him as the source and expose his links to his brothers in-law.

The Menton train pulled in on time. He remained seated and watched as Tim boarded the train. At the last instant he jumped up and also boarded. The journey was only around ten minutes with just two stops. As the train pulled into Menton station, he made sure to be by the doors. Pressing the button to open the doors, he hurried from the train and platform. On exiting the station he instantly saw the Café across the car park. From his visit to Google, he knew that the hotel Belgique was just a hundred metres past the Café on the road to its left.

There were a few diners in the dining room having breakfast, but no-one else to be seen in the Hotel Belgique. He had entered via a glass door into an outer lobby and then into what was the reception area. There was a desk with an open door to the right which led to the dining room. He looked on the reception counter for a bell or something. There were the usual brochures for things to do in the area and a note saying the desk was manned from seven to eleven in the morning and five till nine in the evening. In the dining a room a short black woman appeared carrying breakfasts and placed them on a diner's table.

She saw him "Just a moment," she called as she went behind the bar at the end of the dining room and began to operate the espresso machine. Coffee served she came to the desk. "You were due yesterday evening, two nights," she said.

"Delayed," he had booked for two nights so he would have the room available today. She gave him the key to room fifteen and the code to the front door, should he need to get in after nine in the evening. He paid in cash.

To the left of the desk was a grubby grey, marble spiral staircase. Room fifteen was on the second floor. The grout between the marble tiles on the steps was black and the handrail wobbled as he grabbed it walking upwards. The hotel had its location on its side, directly by the rail Station but very little else. It had been neglected for years. Probably the only time it even approached being full was during the Grand Prix. This was borne out by the diners, who either wore their supported teams logos and colours on their clothing or on their caps. He climbed the stairs to the first floor, paused on the landing and continued up to the top floor of the building.

Room fifteen had a double bed to the left as you entered and a single along the wall at the bottom. A small table, an old chair and a hang rail completed the furnishings. To the right there was a stud wall that didn't reach the ceiling. This contained the smallest basin, toilet and shower known to man. He sat on the chair and considered the turn of events. He placed the two memory sticks on the table. He felt relief at relinquishing them, even if he had only distanced himself from them by a few inches.

He slowly came to the outline of a plan. He looked around the room for a hiding place. He knew, the longer he had the sticks in his possession, the more he was, potentially, providing the smoking gun that would shoot his wife and her brothers. At that moment a train went by, causing the whole room to shake. It galvanised him. He looked around the room for a place to hide them. The usual suspects came to mind - bed, toilet cistern or stuck to the bottom of the table or the chair. All he considered too obvious. His eyes fell on the half closed shutters to the window at the bottom of the bed. Perhaps he should consider outside the room and not in it. He squeezed between the bottom of the bed and the second bed to the Juliet balcony and opened the shutters. He looked around the window opening and gingerly put one foot on the balcony, which he did not trust to support his weight. There was a crack just above his head. It would do. He pushed one stick in, one down one to go. He left leaving the room unlocked.

On his way down he noticed the old stereogram sitting on the mezzanine landing. It presumably had been part of the owners decorating theme, forties retro, or just left over tatty. It had a vase with a bunch of plastic flowers on it. Moving the flowers, he lifted the lid in the centre revealing the turn table. He put the stick on the table, put the lid down, replaced the vase and made his way down and out on to the Rue de la Gare.

Berat turned left as he exited the hotel into the pouring rain and entered the Terminus Café from the side entrance. He could see the Englishman through the glass window sitting on the terrace with his back to the bar. He bought a coffee and swiftly scribbled a note. He pointed out Tim to the owner, handed him the note and an extra ten euros and left. He knew he would have to meet the Englishman at some stage, explain all and trust that his identity would be kept secret.

He stood on the pavement wondering if the Englishman would spot him as he passed the Café and made his way across the car park to the station. While he hesitated, he became aware of the two strangers beside him before he actually saw them. "Stay calm, this is a gun you can feel."

## Chapter 6

Celik had barely left her two brothers. There was a fire going in the waste bin and their computers lay smashed on the floor. The doors flew open and the room was filled with shouting bodies. "Get down, armed police, police, on the floor, hands behind your head."

The shouting continued as Emir and Ahmet had hoods placed over their heads, cuffed and were dragged from the building. They were bundled into the back of a van that then raced through the streets of Istanbul. The next twenty-four hours were a blur. No water, no food, no sleep and no toilet facilities. A plane and another van ride followed.

The hood was pulled off and the handcuffs removed. Emir found himself in a windowless cell with a single light bulb in the centre. The door slammed and he blinked his eyes, dazzled by the brightness, after hours of darkness. His lips were cracked through thirst, his skin hot and parchment like. His body was filthy. His own piss and shit were in his trousers and down his legs that had been rubbed raw through hours of being left sitting in his own excrement.

He noticed a jug of water in the corner on the concrete floor. It just stood there in the bare room. He half crawled and half staggered. Water had never tasted so good. He gulped it down. Too much, too quick, his stomach cramped, twisting like a knife. He vomited. Then more calmly he sipped at the water. Over the next few hours he was left alone, left to let the fear grow inside. The only sound was the occasional loud banging and screaming.

He examined his location. He touched the stained walls,

scrutinising them closely and realising that the stains on the walls were blood. A few pictures, printed on a cheap printer on A4 paper were stuck with sticky tape to the walls. They showed men and women, mostly naked, all had brutally beaten, with broken limbs and smashed and bloody faces. The worm of fear grew.

He sat and waited and waited, the fear growing stronger inside him. He looked at the cracks in the plaster on the walls. His imagination and sleep deprivation causing him to see faces, monstrous faces, in the patterns in the plaster. Some seemed to be smiling, mocking him. He checked the thick wooden door with the stains, dirt and grime engrained in it. He looked for a source of light apart from the yellow dingy light suspended from the single strand of flex, He watched the cockroaches scratchily scamper to and fro, disappearing into cracks in the walls and floors and then reappearing from another. In the background was the constant sound of voices, sometimes raised then interrupted by violent shouting and then moans, wailing and screams. His mind began to take over and imaginings dominated, Nightmare scenarios filled his head, demons from hell, ripping dogs and the walking dead. Lack of food, sleep and isolation forced delirium to the fore.

How long, no way of telling, hours or minutes or day from night. He tried pacing, he tried sleeping, and he tried creating pictures of his family in his head. He tried reciting the Koran and placing his faith in the Prophet, "peace be upon him", but fear still predominated and the isolation continued. No contact, no input, nothing to feed the senses, just the background noise of pain and suffering.

The door slowly opened. Nothing dramatic, no slamming banging or the sudden rush of bodies or clatter, just a small crack that slowly widened. A large Arabic looking man dressed in combat trousers, heavy boots and a black round necked t-shirt lumbered in first. His beard was full, his hair cropped in military fashion. He was a huge man with thick, powerful arms, his neck short, set above massive shoulders. Emir knew that this man was battle harden and had not only seen death but had caused it on many occasions. This man followed orders and would never shirk his duty.

He was followed in by a much smaller man, a dapper man with neatly trimmed hair, a light blue shirt, slacks and slip-on beige shoes. He looked like he was off to the shopping mall or the cinema, or perhaps off to start his daily role as a school teacher. He carried a clip board. They both stood, briefly staring at him huddled in the corner of the room.

The smaller man spoke. He looked down at his clip board and then up at him. "Emir, you do seem to have put yourself in an awkward position. Don't you?" he paused and smiled. "Well I think I may be just the fellow to help you out. Of course, that rather depends if you can help me a little as well. You scratch my back and I will scratch yours"

"Where am I?" Emir found his voice came out as a trembling whisper. He knew he sounded like a whinny schoolgirl.

"I am not at all sure that is important, but in a spirit of the cooperation that I hope will exist between us, I will tell you this. We have a sort of agreement with the Government of your Country to undertake certain tasks. Think of it as outsourcing, a bit like moving the garbage or running a hospital. Yes that is it outsourcing. Your Government has outsourced, to us, the task of asking you some questions. You may ask why they don't do this themselves and I shall answer that question for you."

He paused and looked at Emir. "You do want to know why you have been outsourced, don't you? I am sure you do." answering his own question. "The Americans like to call it rendition, but I prefer the term outsourcing. So, we are recognised leaders in the field of information extraction. It is a simple process. Gather up the subject, in this case you and of course your brother, pop them on a plane to us and just like that we get you the answers you want. "

He continued, "You may ask what the advantage of this

outsourcing is? Again in the spirit, of what I hope will become mutual cooperation, I shall answer that question. You can already see, I hope, what a reasonable man I am? Your Government, I might say, like many other Governments are, quite rightly, firm and staunch upholders of human rights and would under no circumstances use questionable interrogation practices. Turkey, like its allies the United Sates and the United Kingdom and the rest of Europe, which I might add some day hopes to join as a member of the European Union, all therefore do not carry out any such questionable practices. Of course, this would in the normal course of events make it harder and take longer to get answers from the bad men like you and your terrorist buddies."

"Now that both of us know where we stand, I should appreciate it if you would answer a few questions for me?"

Emir said nothing. The large fellow, despite his bulk, took a fast step across the cell and smashed his fist into the centre of his face. His nose cracked, his lips split and blood filled his mouth.

"I think it is important we develop a line of communication. I should appreciate it when I ask a question, that you have at least the good grace to answer. The first question I should like to ask is. Who are you working with?"

This time Emir received a kick to the stomach that forced all the air from his body. He gasped and doubled up and retched, only bringing up bile from a stomach that was completely empty.

"Oh Emir I can see that you are going to be one of those troublesome individuals who would like to experience a great deal of pain before they give me answers to my questions. Given that this is your preferred way for us to proceed, I think it is time that we went a little more high tech, rather than us having my friend here do all this manual stuff like punching and kicking. "

He banged on the door and another military clad figure pushed in a large cabinet on wheels. Emir looked at it. "This is an emergency power supply and you can up and down the voltage etc. state of the art and highly robust. And this is a cattle prod."

The door open again and a chair was brought in. "And this is for me to sit on," he smiled at his own joke. "And this is for you to sit on." This time a much more robust chair was wheeled in with wrist and ankle straps. "Please be so good as to remove your clothes."

Emir didn't move. He was dragged to his feet by the gorilla and stripped. He was dragged from the room and dumped in what passed for a shower where a hose pipe was pointed at him. The freezing cold water made him gasp and the power of the hose was such as to knock him from his feet. He was dragged back and strapped into the chair.

"Now, I hope you feel better after your bath and are sitting comfortably? You could save all this trouble if you just tell me all about it, a few names and the whereabouts of a certain memory stick." Emir said nothing.

Emir screamed. The prod had been first placed on his left nipple then his right. He knew he couldn't survive this for long. He cried, he pleaded, he screamed, but the pain kept on coming.

"I think the penis? Don't you? I am afraid this may affect your chances of having children. Well that is, if you live that is."

Emir passed out.

Emir had been moved while he was unconscious. He awoke to pain everywhere and his brother. This was a different cell, much bigger, with bright lights and more facilities. Water, electricity, a bath, not he guessed used for bathing, chains, hooks and pulleys hung from the ceiling. His brother, Ahmet, was a mess of blood, bruises and broken bones. He was barely conscious and was strapped upright to a large cross against the corner of the cell wall.

"Welcome back Emir" his interrogator spoke softly, as usual, as though they were just having a normal conversation over a cup of tea. "You see, I like to bring families back together," he paused so that Emir could take in the full implications of the sight in front of him.

He raised his hand and the ox, as Emir now thought of the big man who had tortured him for hours, went to the table and opened a box, paused and pulled out a scalpel. Without a word he approached his younger brother's naked body and lifted his penis clear of his scrotum. The knife began to cut into the flesh. One testicle was laid bare of the scrotum and the second revealed in like fashion. His brother was barley aware of what was happening as his testicles were popped, like peas from a pod, from their covering.

Emir heard his voice "Stop, Please stop. I will tell you."

"I knew we could do business, now let's begin. No time like the present, as time is pressing. Would you like something to eat and drink, perhaps, as we proceed?"

## Chapter 7

Mehmet, deputy head of Turkish security, was aboard the Lady Heloise in Monte Carlo. He and his entourage were gathered in the private stateroom. The conversation was constantly interrupted by the roar of the cars. Mehmet sat at the head of the circular, glossy, rosewood table. "Where is he?"

The rest of the officials looked at each other nervously. Yosuf replied with some trepidation. "Gone, disappeared, he left early this morning and hasn't returned."

"Get out, all of you and ask Jason Delonge if he could spare me a few moments of his valuable time."

Jason arrived and he and Mehmet sat opposite each other. "How are you my friend?"

"Fine Mo and you?" asked Jason.

"I need a little help and I think you are the man to help," he paused to let Jason know that this was not a request but a demand.

"Of course."

"This morning I received news that an interpreter who works for us, has a certain something in his possession that we should like."

"I don't understand, what has your interpreter to do with me?"

"You will. His name is Berat and some associates of ours have been talking to his brothers in-law. These men are bad men,

186

terrorists, members of ISIS and they gave Berat something which we should like back. A USB memory stick in fact and when we received this information we went and searched Berat's room at the hotel and it was not there, nor was he. We did not find the stick, but we did find an email to you."

Jason knew he had a problem. This was obviously something he had to hand over to British Intelligence and he could not hand it over to a Foreign Government. He also knew that Tim had failed to meet with this Berat and he did not have the stick in his possession as yet. "Why do you need it, surely you can let MI6 deal with it?"

"My Government wants the credit, you understand, for this. It would be a major coup for us in the fight against terror."

"I cannot help you," Jason got up to leave.

"Oh! But I think you can and you will." Mehmet turned the laptop round that had been facing him on the desk. There was a video image of Jason and the small boy with the big oval eyes.

Jason Delonge stared unbelieving at the screen as he had hoped never to see that face again. He thought back to that summer five years ago. He had not been surprised to receive the invite from Mo. They had been firm friends at University and they had travelled to North Africa together, smoking dope and buggering the young men during the summer recess. Of course, Jason had given up the dope, but not the buggery and was well on his way to a career as a diplomat. Mehmet Yildirim's, Mo's, career had also progressed since their time at University. He was looking forward to seeing his old friend again and there was always the opportunity to swap a bit of intelligence that had the potential to be helpful to both their careers. The plane touched down on time and with his diplomatic passport, Jason was soon sat comfortably in the back of the black Mercedes, sipping a glass of champagne, as the driver struggled with the traffic in Istanbul.

The villa was incredible, the automatic gates rolled open to reveal a sweeping cypress tree lined drive that wound its way to the house. Jason liked to describe the architecture as Middle East, over the top, bling. The big double doors were opened by the butler onto the marble clad vestibule with a double staircase curving upwards to the galleried landing. The biggest gold and crystal chandelier hung the full two stories from the domed ceiling that was panelled in decorative, painted glass. Even Jason had to admit this was bling on a whole new level. Every nook and cranny was stuffed with antique furniture, gold objects d'art and tapestry works. Even the old Sultans would have been given a run for their money in this place.

As is the nature of Turkish tradition, the house was more or less segregated between the public and the private. You did business in one and the family lived in the other. The house was arranged around a beautiful tiled, central square garden with a bubbling fountain that issued clear, sparkling water. Obviously, the owner did not feel the need to stick with any particular style of architecture and had not minded adding a bit of Moroccan into the mix. It was totally over the top, but, if not demonstrating the taste of the owner, it certainly demonstrated his wealth,

"Jason, so glad to see you," Mo crossed the thick pile of the traditionally patterned, hand woven carpet of the library. The walls lined with volume after volume of leather bound and hand tooled books, Light streamed in from an ornate window at the end with verses from the Koran etched around it.

"Mo. It has been too long. What a beautiful place." said Jason.

"Not mine old boy, a friend's. In fact there are a couple of people who I should like you to meet after you have had a wash and brush up. They will join us for diner. Just the usual business types looking for introductions in the UK and a nod of approval," Jason was not surprised, after all, there was no such thing as a free lunch.

Dinner was quite a formal affair. There were eighteen, including his host and himself, all men of wealth. The table was magnificent, gold cutlery, finest crystal and fine dining. "Mr Delonge," said the gentleman to his left. "I understand that you and Mehmet went to Oxford together?"

"We did indeed and Eton of course."

"The finest school in the world, I am hoping for my son also to go. Firm friendships are built on such experiences. Friendship is so important, don't you agree?" Jason agreed. "Such friendships last a lifetime and can be so helpful in meeting the right people, the right circle, and the right network."

He paused and stared at Jason, trying to gauge his state of receptiveness. Jason smiled and nodded knowingly. This encouraged him to continue. "Perhaps after we have sampled this delicious meal you, me and a few of my colleagues could discuss some sort of arrangement?"

Jason decided to not let this go all one sided and he knew enough to make the play a little difficult. It would all add to the price at the end of it, he did not want to appear to be too cheap. "What sort of arrangement?"

"Oh nothing formal, of course, we respect your position and neutrality, but perhaps there are areas of mutual benefit we could explore."

The meal had been sumptuous and Jason could not help but notice how the small boys, aged no more than nine or ten, had scurried around helping the serving staff. As he settled in an armchair in the library, a dark haired boy with large oval eyes and long eye lashes passed him a glass of Remy Martin from a silver tray held by the butler. He smiled and looked away shyly.

The discussions went very well and Jason had added significantly to his annual income and would, in return, provide ad-hoc consultancy to his new business acquaintances. He settled back in the armchair. The guests having left, he and Mo sat facing each other. "Do you remember those weeks in Morocco?" asked Mo.

"Never to be forgotten. Good to be young with no commitments."

"Ah yes, commitments, they do have a habit of cutting down life's pleasures." He beckoned the boy, who had served Jason earlier and gently stroked his head. "It is a shame these commitments." He waved the boy away. "Goodnight, I think."

Jason made his way to his suite of rooms. A bathroom in gold and marble, a dressing room, a lounge with a bar, a television the size of a cinema screen and a huge bed completed the accommodation. He discarded his clothes and headed for the shower. The water was warm and ran down his body. He wondered if there might be a porn channel on the television. He felt his penis begin to harden. He stroked it up and down in the shower using the soap as lube. He continued rubbing gently up and down until it was fully erect. "A nice wank over a bit of porn on the TV and he would get a good night's sleep," he thought as he made his way from the bathroom.

At first he was startled, there was someone in the room and his heart jumped. Sitting on the bed was the small boy with the oval eyes and soft olive coloured skin. He looked tiny sat in the middle of the huge bed naked.

The screen on Mehmet's laptop now displayed what the secret camera had caught in that room five years ago.

## Chapter 8

Yosuf had seen that look in Mehmet's eyes once or twice before. Mehmet, he knew was a fanatic in his own way but not a religious zealot, nor a man of principle. He was, in fact, more of a sadist with an incurable drive to inflict pain. The job he had allowed him full licence to his passions, including torture, rape, paedophilia and murder. He felt his stomach knot and the hairs on the back of his neck rise as he met Mehmet's stare.

He knew he was dead. It was only a question of how and when and how much pain was to come. On balance, Yosuf thought that he would be allowed to travel back to Turkey so he could quietly disappear. Killing him here in France could bring messy complications, as the French were not that keen on people dumping bodies along the Cote D'Azure.

He had worked with Berat for six or seven years. He knew him. He was a good man, a decent man, who worked hard at his job and a good Muslim. When he heard that Berat's brothers in-law were to be arrested and were involved with ISIS, he just wanted to warn Berat so he could make sure that he and Celik distanced themselves and cleaned their house, so to speak, to double check they had nothing, nothing at all to link them to the terrorists. He should have known better, for the very reasons he had warned him.

He had been stupid and with hindsight he should have known that Berat would, being the man he was, try and protect his family. Now it was all too late, events had led him and Berat, both of them, to certain imprisonment or death. His mind raced. "What were his options?"

He knew he had but one choice, run. He hurried to the cabin set aside at the rear of the Yacht for communications. The amount of equipment was small, a powerful computer, a printer and a guard on the door. They could encrypt and send secure messages and scramble the phone, allowing them to communicate with home with relative immunity from being listened to or hacked. The cabin had been swept for listening devices so it also afforded the opportunity for very private conversations. The cabin also acted as a secure location for their confidential possessions, bags, laptops and files, the things you would not leave in a hotel room.

As he descended to the secure cabin, he considered Berat's actions. He realised, that once Berat's wife had warned her brothers and become involved by taking the evidence against them he, Berat, being a decent man, had needed to do something. He should have destroyed the evidence, but his conscience would not let him. He could not hand it over to Mehmet as that would have been tantamount to handing his wife over for torture and providing a death warrant for her brothers. Knowing that he had a piece of evidence that could potentially save countless lives, Berat had wanted to get that information into the hands of someone who would use it, but not against his wife and family. So he had contacted the British. He had not foreseen that his brother in-law would have cracked under torture and given up his sister. Nor could he have foreseen that the Brit he contacted would be a paedophile buddy of Mehmet's. In fact, as soon as Celik became involved, it had only been a matter of time before he was in the firing line. Yosuf was also pretty damn sure that ISIS by would be sniffing him out soon as well. Turkish security leaked like a sieve. There was a great deal of support for a return to fundamentalism all across society and Government Departments were not isolated from society as a whole.

The guard smiled broadly at Yosuf, as he recognised him. They had travelled all over together and were friends, "How's the race going?"

"Hamilton has the lead and provided nothing goes wrong with his car he should take the win."

"You have all the luck, pretty women and fast cars. I just get to stand down here watching the luggage," he opened the door for Yosuf.

He entered and closed the door behind him. He had, at the bottom of his heart, known it might always have come to this. He had rehearsed it a thousand times in his head. Planned every move, but had never really expected it to become a reality. His hands trembled as he picked up the oversized bag. It was the type that accountants and lawyers used to carry their clients documents. Black, sturdy and leather clad, it was a cross between a big box and a carry-on luggage bag. It bore the diplomatic emblem and seal. These bags either travelled with their owners at all times, with the capability to be handcuffed to them, or they travelled in the hold of a plane in large, sealed, metal boxes. In any event, it was part of the diplomatic mission and immune from customs or any other form of border scrutiny. Guns, drugs and even people had been transported using this convention.

As Yosuf had risen in the ranks, he had become more and more aware of how perilous a career could be in a Country that seemed to be going backwards on human rights. He had started to slip things in his bag over the years. It had become a full flight and survival kit. Passports, money, IDs, it had built up over the years. He took his bag and tapped on the door to be let out, "You are not the only one to miss the race, the lowlier of us have work still to do," he quipped with the guard as he left.

There would be no going back, he knew that, he also knew that going back to Turkey would be injurious to his health and potentially, fatal. The party was now in full swing. A black girl and her friend were doing a striptease for the lads and he knew a couple of the prostitutes were conducting a gang bang in a cabin in the bowels of the boat. All good fun to lubricate the spirit of international friendship,

He had one small matter he wanted to satisfy himself on before he went. He spotted Ahmed, the gofer, with the other porters and valets congregated in a small group watching the two strippers, now rubbing and playing with each other, putting on the lesbian finale to their show before they moved to join the other prostitutes to do their fucking duty downstairs. He carefully pushed his bag under the buffet table and made his way over to the group.

"Met," he said, gesturing for him to come over to him. He was known to all and referred to as "Met the bag," for obvious reasons. "Can you tell me something?" he asked. Met nodded in response "Did you load up the British contingent at the hotel and ship them down here?"

"Yes, I always take personal charge of the foreigners, better to have a fuck up with your own group than balls up the guests transport, why? Is there a problem?"

"No, no problem, but tell me, did they all make the limos?"

Met rummaged through his pockets and pulled out a piece of paper. "My list, it is like a school trip. I count them on the way here and count them out on the way back. That way I don't leave any lying around anywhere." He smiled as he looked down at his list.

"Only one, Anthony Burr, made his own way here."

"Thank you," he said. Yosuf knew who Anthony Burr was and decided to have a wander around and take a look for him, before discreetly picking his moment and disappearing

## Chapter 9

The ISIS banner, with its bold lettering in white on its black background, hung from the wall. The hooded figure moved from the camera's field of vision revealing the tableau behind. The computer screen filled as the web cam was moved in closer

"Do you recognise that cunt?"

The screen showed a close up of the female genitalia. A hand appeared from out of shot and roughly began to probe the labia, seeking the entry. The camera pulled back unsteadily, showing more of the scene.

The lower half a naked woman's body was stretched across a table, her legs tied to the legs of the table exposing the hair of her pubic region, the hooded figure probing and pulling roughly. She was completely naked. The hooded figure held his erect penis in his other hand, he was rubbing it vigorously.

The camera widened its angle further and her naked body, in its entirety, was exposed, her breast slipping slightly to the side of her chest. One was being fondled by a second hooded male, also exposing his erect penis. The camera hovered above her chest.

"Infidel whore," was written across her chest and stomach in Arabic.

"Fuck the whore," the voice said. "Such bitches are there to serve you, the sons of Jihad. She is not human. She is scum that floats to the surface when confronted by the truths of Islam." The rant continued in the same vain, becoming almost hysterical as she was fucked. She was pounded with no regard for her body, "Fuck the whore and fuck her hard."

Celik had just popped down to the shops when the van stopped in the street. Before she had a chance to respond, she had been dragged into the back, gagged and hooded. No one reported it. Then the hell had begun. She had been taken to this filthy room and raped hour after hour. "Filthy whore, fuck the whore, fuck the slut's cunt, fuck her arse." It continued and continued. She screamed, she pleaded, she bled and her body tore.

"See how your slut wife enjoys it." Rough hands forced Berat to look at the screen. Berat had been marched back to room fifteen in the Hotel Belgique. He was pinned to the chair by two individuals with a knife to his throat. Tears ran down his cheeks as he struggled frantically to free himself. He was no match for his captors. He could not cry out, his mouth stuffed with the towel from the bathroom. He slumped forward. He had lost the will to fight. He could not bear to watch his beautiful wife being used like a piece of meat any longer. He looked up at his captors, pleading, a broken man.

His captor removed the gag, "well?

He gasped in air, "On the balcony, in the crack above the window."

His tormentor moved to the balcony and pushed the shutters open and looked above him. There it was. "It is here," he confirmed to his companions. The knife was drawn across Berat's throat and there was a gasp and a cough as the three left room fifteen.

Printed in Great Britain
by Amazon